STRIKE ZONE

The Games Of Baseball & Money

S. L. Hudson

S. L. Hudson

CreateSpace

For information or permissions contact:
S.L.Hudson@StrikeZone-TheBook.com

Books are available at special discounts for bulk
purchases in the United States. Please contact
S.L.Hudson@StrikeZone-TheBook.com

Cover: concept by S. L. Hudson, graphic design by
Robyn Hepker of Benson & Hepker Design

First Edition

ISBN 1449553818
EAN-13 9781449553814

CreateSpace is a member of
the Amazon group of companies

Dedicated to the memory of
Theodore Martin Chermak

Those who knew him
will hear his voice within *Strike Zone*.

CONTENTS

CHAPTER ONE
THE AIDA CODE

Without opening his eyes, Dan ran his hand along the edge of his pillow in search of his baseball glove. He felt the supple leather, and reached into its pocket to retrieve his favorite baseball. Rolling on his back, he began to massage the curve of the baseball with a mesmerizing rhythm, at times suspending it between the tips of his fingers and at other times nearly hiding it in the palms of his hands.

He never seemed to tire of the feel of the cool smooth leather and the contrasting ridges of the stitching. Dan practiced placing his fingers precisely on the stitches as if he were pitching his fastball, then his curve, and finally his slider. His finger placement had become automatic. He knew the exact formation of the baseball's red stitches, even with his eyes shut. He smiled with satisfaction.

Opening his eyes, Dan began tossing the baseball across his chest from his right hand to his left and back again. With each toss, his energy grew as he envisioned himself as his freshman team's starting pitcher at the state tournament. That was his goal, and he was prepared to work hard to reach it. He could hardly wait to meet the new assistant coaches that Coach Tisdale said would begin working with the team today.

He swung his feet over the edge of the bed. As he did, he caught a glimpse of the carton of chocolate bars on the floor near his dresser. His emotions dropped with the speed of a roller coaster. Dan groaned, and rolled back into bed, pulling the sheet over his head. His thoughts were no longer on the game of baseball.

At today's practice, he knew he would have to report on the money he had raised for his freshman team to go the state finals. The season was just starting. Even so, the team had agreed they were going to end the season by going to the tournament in Des Moines, and they didn't intend to be spectators.

Dan pulled his knees to his chest, wrapped his arms around them, and began to rock back and forth. His chocolate bar sales had been dismal. When he voted to raise the money that way, it seemed like a good idea. He didn't know then it would be so hard. By this morning he was supposed to have sold an entire carton of chocolate bars, and he hadn't even managed to sell a whole box. He had sold only 15 bars, and if the truth be known, 8 of those he had bought for himself.

The last time he felt like this was when he had a book report due, and he hadn't read the book. Only this was worse, much worse. With the book report, he hadn't even tried, but he had tried to sell the chocolate bars. He had knocked on neighbors' doors, and even stopped them on the street. He sold a few, but nowhere near enough. He had failed. Failed the team, failed Coach Tisdale, failed himself.

Dan tried to think of something that would make him look better when he had to report his failure to his team members. He considered using his allowance to buy the whole carton, but then realized that was a dumb decision. The team's game plan called for each player to sell one carton of chocolate bars each week, for three weeks.

Dan might not be good at sales, but he was a whiz with math. That was an easy calculation. Three cartons. Twelve boxes per carton. Twenty-four chocolate bars per box. One dollar per chocolate bar. No way, he didn't have enough savings.

A sudden blast of music from his older brother's room interrupted Dan's thoughts. He could feel the bass vibrate the wall between his and Grant's bedroom. Loud music didn't really bother Dan, but he knew it bothered his mom, and he figured this was an opportunity to balance the scorecard between him and Grant.

He clenched his fist and walloped the wall. To make sure his protest was heard in the kitchen, he bellowed, "Quiet!" at the top of his lungs. Then he pulled his pillow to his chest and smirked with satisfaction as he waited for Mom to come storming up the stairs and issue Grant a "sound-out" for the rest of the day—maybe two days if he was lucky.

Dan was still mad at his older brother for teasing him about being better at eating his inventory than selling it. Just because Grant was in college didn't give him the right to put his nose where it didn't belong. What business was it of his that Dan was eating his inventory, anyway? He paid for them after all. In spite of their age difference, and little bickers like this, the Martin brothers were close and defended each other against all comers, but they still hassled one another. They both kept track of slights, and each was constantly working to balance the scorecard they carried in their heads.

Grant cranked up the sound. It wasn't the kind of music that Grant usually played. It was probably some new college thing. Dan banged on the wall again. Where was Mom? Then the music stopped. "Hey, Sport," Grant called. "Stop the bangin' and drag your old bod in here."

Dan's first impulse was to bang louder, but he reconsidered. He was seldom invited into Grant's room, so he decided to take advantage of the opportunity. It might have something to do with Grant moving to Omaha for his summer intern job. He decided to balance his scorecard later.

Grant's bedroom door was open. Dan glanced at the POSTED, NO TRESPASSING, and PASSPORTS REQUIRED signs that Grant had glued on his door when he was in junior high.

"Just listen to this," Grant said. He hit the remote to restart the CD. A big brassy sound filled the room. Grant waved his arms in the air pretending to conduct a few bars.

"What's with the music? It doesn't sound much like you."

Grant eyeballed Dan at close range. "That is your first lesson in how to sell your chocolate bars."

"I don't get the connection. What's music got to do with selling chocolate bars?"

"That, my man, was no ordinary music. That was the march from *Aida*."

"You mean Mom's opera? What's that got to do with selling chocolate bars?"

"Nothing and everything," Grant whispered mysteriously, rolling his eyes.

Dan found that look both annoying and exciting. Annoying because he could never guess what Grant was up to, and exciting because it usually meant something fun. Grant played the march from *Aida* again and proclaimed, "That should be the theme song of every entrepreneur."

"What's an entrepreneur?"

"That's what you are."

"I am?"

"Absolutely."

"Absolutely?"

"Absolutely!"

Dan wasn't going to ask. He just looked at Grant, who finally said, "Did you or did you not agree to accept the challenge from your team and Coach Tisdale to sell three cartons of chocolate bars?"

Dan just continued to stare at him.

"Well, don't just sit there like a bump on a log. Did you or didn't you?"

"Yeah, I guess so, but ..."

"Right, you accepted the challenge. Now, it's up to you to find a creative way to meet that challenge. Coach Tisdale has made an investment in you, and now you have a responsibility to give him a return on investment."

"I have no idea what you're talking about."

Grant continued. "You don't think that someone just walked up to Coach Tisdale and said, 'Hey Ted, you're a great guy. So, I've decided to *give* you 75 cartons of chocolate bars, so your team can raise some money to go to the state baseball tournament?' Not too likely, even if the wholesale chocolate dealer was a Roughrider fan. Coach probably still had to shell out a pretty penny to get that inventory."

Dan was starting to get the idea. "I never thought about that."

"Well, think about it now. Coach Tisdale took a calcu-lated risk in trying to find a way to raise some quick money so you nerds could go to the state tournament. Whether his investment was a good one, or a bad one, de-pends on you and the rest of the team. If you guys sell the chocolate bars, it's a good investment. If you don't, ... your choice."

Dan squirmed. "Yeah, well, just because you've been studying business in college and know everything doesn't mean I do."

"Stuff it. All ya gotta do is use your gray matter. Do you want to sell those chocolate bars or not?"

"Yeah, I want to sell the bars, but no one wants to buy them."

"No one? Just who have you asked?"

"You, Mom, Mr. Mercer, Mrs. Blum, the Andersons, the Gallos, ... I mean, I've asked everyone."

"Well, at least you've asked everyone that lives on our street. But there's a whole big world out there beyond our little street."

"Maybe, but I don't know them."

"You don't have to know them, man. You aren't inviting them to dinner. All you need to do is offer to let them buy one of your chocolate bars. Tell me this, are they good chocolate bars?"

"Yeah."

"Do you enjoy eating them?"

"Shove it!" Dan bristled, recalling Grant's remarks about eating the inventory.

Grant gave Dan's belly a pat or two. Dan whacked him with a pillow.

Grant laughed and continued, "Do you think other people could enjoy eating them?"

"Sure."

"Would you like to sell all those chocolate bars?"

"No, but I'd like to have sold them." Dan smiled at his clever retort.

"Yeah, yeah, that's what I meant, Mr. Wise Guy. Would it feel good to take all that money to Coach Tisdale?"

"You bet."

"Would you like to go to the state tournament?"

"That's a dumb question."

"Well, then, give me a smart answer."

"Yes, I want to go to the state tournament!"

Grant put the march from *Aida* on again. "That's how!"

"I still don't see how a march from one of Mom's operas will sell those stinkin' chocolate bars."

"You're right, a march won't sell chocolate bars, but I'll bet you a shiny Arbor Day quarter the lesson I'm gonna teach you about the AIDA code will, and you'll never forget it."

"I don't get this … you're just nuts or something."

"You'll get it, you'll get it, hang in there. How do you spell AIDA?"

"I-E-D-A?"

"That's how it sounds, but it's really spelled A-I-D-A."

"This whole thing is soundin' nuts."

"Come on, Dan, give it a chance. Are you happy with your sales this week?

"Of course not. You think I'm stupid?"

"Well, if you keep doing things the same old way, you can expect to get the same old results."

"Okay, okay, I'm listenin', I'm listenin'."

"Good. A-I-D-A will be our secret code that will help you remember some important things that will help you sell your chocolate bars. It's really an acronym. For example, I've been advertising my consulting services to you. First came the 'A'. I got your *Attention*. I turned up my

CD player to the max, and then I invited you into my room. Then I started conducting. I got your attention. Right?"

"Right!"

"Then came the 'I.' I had to hold your *Interest*. I started throwing out big words like entrepreneur, investment, and calculated risk. I also tried to create a puzzle around AIDA. I know you love puzzles. Were you interested?"

"Yeah, I guess so."

"Then I had to raise your *Desire*, so I focused on your competitive spirit and your sense of fair play. I knew you wouldn't want to let Coach Tisdale down, and I also knew you really, really want to go to the state tournament. Am I battin' a thousand?"

"You're battin' better than Babe Ruth, but I still don't see how I'm gonna to sell those chocolate bars."

"Cool it, we haven't yet covered the final 'A'. If I want you to be my client, I must give you a call for *Action*. So, if you want to hear more, follow me to the war room and we'll discuss an action plan. "

Grant straight-armed Dan in the chest and toppled him back on the bed. Grant raced for the bedroom door. Dan rebounded from the bed, caught up with Grant, and tried to edge him out as they raced down the stairs. They jostled one another at every opportunity. Grant didn't cut Dan any slack just because he was younger. That just wasn't the Martin family way. Grant slipped through the basement door first and pulled it closed behind him. Dan gave the door a whack, just as the hall clock chimed the quarter hour.

"Put this on hold, I'm gonna be late for practice." Dan did a quick about face, sprinted up the stairs to his room, grabbed his glove, slid down the banister, and raced out the kitchen door. Mounting his bike like a bronco rider, he was on his way before the kitchen door slammed.

CHAPTER TWO
THE FABULOUS FOUR

Some of the sweat that formed on Dan's forehead and upper lip was the result of his exertion, but most was the result of the anxiety he was feeling that he might be late for practice. As he approached the slope to the *Talking Tree,* he slammed on his brakes, dismounted, and sprinted up the hill, letting the bike wobble to the ground on its own. Just as Coach Tisdale blew his whistle, Dan slid into his self-designated spot among his closest friends, Chandler, Spider, and Gabby.

The *Talking Tree* didn't talk, of course, but it was magic, or at least he and his friends liked to think it was. For nearly 40 years, Coach Tisdale had gathered his teams under its branches to share bits of wisdom about baseball, and about life. When Dan's dad and older brother, Grant, had played for the Roughriders, they had sat in the exact spot that Dan now occupied.

Spaces under the *Talking Tree* were not assigned, yet each player had a spot he considered his. Grant had told Dan that if he wanted to claim the "family spot," all he would have to do is arrive for practice early for the first week and sit in that spot. From then on, he'd own it. Grant called it "personal territory." He said it was a psychological thing. Dan didn't care what it was called as long as it worked.

The players also had their special spots on the team bench. Dan always sat with his friends and they always sat in the same order, tallest on the left to the shortest on the right. They always walked in that order also, unless they were in single file, then Gabby who was the shortest, always went first. Considering his "me-first" personality, that wasn't too surprising.

Dan's dad had snapped a photo of them in their signature formation at last year's final ballgame, and had a poster of it made for Dan's birthday. The caption read: *Roosevelt Roughriders. The Fabulous Four. Charles "Chandler" Curtis, Dan "Big D" Martin, Miguel "Spider" Hernandez, Patrick "Gabby" Sullivan.* It was one of Dan's most valued possessions, and the last present his dad had given him.

Dan enjoyed always sitting between Chandler and Spider, but he knew it wasn't just a kid thing. Lots of parents and regular fans had a habit of arriving early for games to lay claim to their favorite spots in the bleachers. He could understand that. He knew he always was irritated if anyone sat in one of "his" spots.

Today however, he would have taken any spot without complaint. He was thrilled that he wasn't late to practice.

"Courtin' trouble?" Spider whispered from the corner of his mouth.

"Later," Dan gulped as he sucked in air. His timing had been off. He'd never cut it so close. He hadn't planned on Grant's invitation, or the AIDA thing. Man, if he hadn't heard the clock chime on the way to the war room, he definitely would have been late for practice—might have even missed it altogether.

Coach had some ironclad rules, and punctuality was at the top of the list. Roosevelt athletes were never late. It just didn't happen. Everyone knew Ted Tisdale wasn't one for excuses. Coach made sure his players knew his rules, and what to expect if they broke them. That didn't mean he was rigid or that things were always the same, but he did have some traditions.

Coach started every practice with a special chant. Today was no exception.

"Who are you?" Coach barked.

In unison the team responded, "Roosevelt Roughriders."

"What's your vision?"

"To be the best we can be."

"... and your values?"

"Honesty! Integrity! Fair play!"

Dan learned the chant when he was still in grade school, when he came to watch Grant practice. He had no idea what he was yelling about then, but now, maybe because he was older, or maybe because he was now a team member, he made the effort to understand what the words meant.

Coach Tisdale picked up his clipboard. "Listen up. This is important. To be the best you can be, you have to play with the best. Got that?"

"Yes, sir!" They yelled back, their stomach muscles powering each word.

"There's the best." He pointed his thumb over his shoulder to where the varsity team was warming up. "They're the champions! Those are the guys that have set the standard for what our community expects from you." Coach paused to let that sink in.

"You're selling chocolate bars to raise money to go to the state tournament. Whether you'll be on the field competing, or just in the stands as an observer, is up to you. Those players out there on the field are the reigning state champions. You owe it to them to *think* like champions.

You owe it to Roosevelt to *play* like champions. You owe it to yourselves to *be* champions. Each one of you must step up and fill one of those guys' shoes."

A huge cheer filled the air and reverberated off the school's walls.

Dan looked toward the pitcher's mound. How could anyone fill Bob Carlsen's shoes? Carlsen was the best pitcher Roosevelt had seen since his dad was a student. Carlsen was a natural. Everybody said so. Dan's feeling of insecurity began to grow. Suddenly he realized he had missed something.

"Isn't that right, Martin?" Coach Tisdale demanded.

"Yes, sir," Dan barked back, knowing "yes" was the right answer, but having no idea what preceded the question.

Having recaptured Dan's attention, Coach Tisdale continued. "If you're going to be the best, you must field like champions, bat like champions, and make split-second decisions like champions. Got that?"

"Yes, sir," the team responded.

"Good. Remember what I said when I started. If you want to be the best, you need to play with the best. The varsity team will play against you two games a week, straight through to tournament time. They won't be cutting you any slack. They intend to beat you every game if they can. However, this is not about winning. This is about learning. Learning to be the best you can be. Learning to play like champions. Got that?"

Spider elbowed Dan in the ribs. "Bummer," he whispered, "who wants to lose two games a week?"

Dan gave him a frown and snapped his head in Coach Tisdale's direction. Spider made an exasperated sigh.

Tisdale turned his megaphone toward the varsity team. "All right, Champs. We're ready to start. Take your positions."

The varsity players mobilized themselves. There were at least two men at every position, three in some. Coach turned toward his freshman players. "Each one of you has been paired with a player from the varsity team. They are my new assistant coaches. So go to the position you normally play to meet the player I have assigned to be your personal coach."

"This is crazy!" Gabby complained as they hustled toward the diamond. "Why would the team we're playing against want to help us improve our game?"

"Give it a chance," Chandler said to no one in particular. The four friends parted at the pitcher's mound. Gabby switched back to home plate. Spider headed to shortstop and Chandler ran out to center field. Dan stood at the base of the pitcher's mound nervously slamming his right fist into the pocket of his glove.

When everyone was in position, Coach Tisdale continued. "All right, Champs, you know the player you've been assigned to coach. Take him aside and study his warm-up exercises. Make a mental note of where improvements are needed. Choose one exercise and kaizen it. Got it?"

"Yes, sir," thundered the two teams in unison.

Dan "Yes, sir'd" right along with everyone else, but he had never heard of a kaizen, and he hadn't the slightest idea how to kaizen anything.

Bob Carlsen put his arm around Dan's shoulder. "Okay, Martin, let's show 'em how it's done."

Dan's mood changed immediately. Wow! Bob Carlsen, the varsity captain, had been assigned as his personal coach. He couldn't believe his luck. Last season Carlsen had led his freshman team to the state championship. Everyone talked about how he was one of the best athletes Roosevelt had ever seen.

"All right!" Dan exclaimed. Carlsen sauntered toward the area outside the third base line. Dan followed, with every step he felt like he was walking on springs.

"You planin' on coming to our game tomorrow?" Carlsen asked.

"Haven't missed a varsity opener since I was old enough to walk."

"Terrific! We need the energy of a good crowd to keep us on our toes."

"You're always on your toes. Pressure doesn't seem to faze you."

"Thanks, but looks can be deceiving. I definitely feel the pressure. But Coach has taught me a few things to help me get past it."

"Will you teach me?"

"I'm not sure I know exactly what happens inside my head when I'm in a tight spot, but Coach says confidence has a lot to do with it, so he has me doing things that'll build my confidence."

"Like what?"

"Training my muscle memory, for one."

"Can you teach me to do that?"

"No, but you can teach yourself. It just takes practice, practice, practice until your moves are automatic; you don't even think about it. It just comes natural."

"Is that what they mean when they say 'you're a natural'"?

"I don't think any athlete is a natural. Some guys work so hard at training their mind and body they just seem to do what they do without effort, but believe me, they've put in the hours practicing and studying their game to make it look that way."

"So, what specifically?"

Carlsen smiled, "Practice, practice, practice. Pay attention to the little things. I study the game a lot. I watch other pitchers a lot. I try to learn from their smart decisions, as well as their dumb ones."

"Yeah, I know what you mean; I do that too."

"Great, at our next practice, you can give me a critique of tomorrow night's game. That way we can kinda coach each other."

"I'm still learnin' how to pitch, I don't know a thing about coaching."

"You know more than you think."

"I know it's a lot less painful to problem-solve another pitcher's mistakes than it is my own."

Carlsen smiled and snapped his fist into the pocket of his glove. "What da'ya say we work on your muscle memory? Let me see your warm-up routine."

Dan wasn't much for warm-ups. They were soooo boring. The same old thing over and over. He started with some leg stretches, followed by toe touches, moved on to body benders, and finished off with deep knee bends.

Carlsen didn't say a word until Dan finished. Then he asked, "What would you like to kaizen?"

"What's that mean, anyway?"

"What? Kaizen?"

"Yeah."

"Aw, it's just a Japanese word that Coach likes to use," Carlsen explained. "It means to do something just a little bit better than you did it the day before. Take your leg stretches, for example. You're good at them, but you could be even better."

"I already did ten," Dan complained, "but I suppose I could do five more."

"Yeah, or you could do five less. It's not about the numbers. It's about doing what you do more effectively."

"How would I do them more ... effectively?" Dan liked repeating "effectively." It made him feel older, more sophisticated.

"Give more flex to your knee. Get your shin more horizontal to the ground," Carlsen instructed.

"Like this?"

"Naw, I think you need to change your stance just before you step forward into your stretch. Start by balancing with your feet about 6 inches apart." Dan followed Carlsen's instructions.

"Good. Now take a step to the right, flex your knee a little, and shift all your weight to that right foot." Carlsen nodded his approval as Dan did as he was told. "Keep that leg flexed, and do the same with your other leg."

Dan could immediately feel a difference in his leg muscles.

"Now, put your arms out in front of you about waist high."

It felt awkward.

"Good. Turn your palms down. Perfect! You look just like King Kong. Now step forward into your stretch."

Dan moved slowly, but deliberately.

"Notice how your body has a little side slant that wasn't there before, and how much more horizontal to the ground your back leg is? How does that feel?"

After Dan returned to his new King Kong stance, he raised his arms and beat his chest with his fists. He let go some deep guttural King Kong bellows. Some of the nearby players paused in their workouts to see what was going on. Carlsen chuckled and offered Dan a high five.

Chandler was right, Dan thought, we should give this "play with the best thing" a chance. This could be sweet, real sweet.

After warm-ups, the two teams played three practice innings. Nobody was supposed to be keeping score, but everyone did in his own mind. The varsity trounced them. Gabby definitely was not having a good practice. He made three errors. Coach finally took mercy and blew his whistle. "Take five and meet me under the *Talking Tree.*"

Dan, Gabby, Chandler, and Spider raced up the slope toward the *Talking Tree.*

"Make way!" Spider demanded, stiff-arming Dan as he passed him.

"You're goin' nowhere!" Dan grabbed the tail of Spider's tee, slowing him down. Spider swiveled and broke free by delivering a karate chop to Dan's pitching arm. "Cheap shot," Dan complained.

Spider turned and thumbed his nose at the others. As he did so, his foot slipped on a loose rock, and he tumbled to the ground. Dan managed to sidestep him, but Chandler, who was close behind, wasn't as lucky. He uncharacteristically tripped on Spider's out-flung leg. On his way down, Chandler managed to lunge and grab Dan's foot.

"Way to go, Chandler," Gabby cheered as he caught up. Dan was still standing, so Gabby delivered him a shoulder block. "This race is mine," he shouted as he took the lead. Instead of knocking Dan off balance, Gabby had unintentionally provided the extra force Dan needed to free his foot. Chandler was left holding an empty shoe.

Gabby, thinking the other three were down, slowed a little. Not much, just a little, but it cost him the race. Dan managed to tag the ancient oak tree a split second before him.

"Alright!" Gabby cheered for himself. "I almost won."

"When a turtle can sprint," Dan countered.

Gabby ignored him. He began bouncing from one foot to the other and popping his baseball into his mitt with the regularity of a metronome. Finally he blurted out, "How'd everybody do? How'd ya do? How'd ya do? Did you sell all your chocolate bars?"

Chandler, Spider, and Dan tackled him and the foursome tumbled about in friendly camaraderie. Coach blew his whistle and ran his thumb and forefinger along the brim of his baseball cap. "Those of you who think you're football players, report to Coach Yanachek. Those of you who think you're baseball players, listen up!"

All eyes shifted to the foursome. Someone started a long low "OO-oo-oo," and others joined in. The accusatory wave drifted out across the diamond. The foursome shifted uneasily in their places. When Coach felt his point had sunk in he said, "Alright men, how have we been doing on our chocolate bar sales?"

Dan felt a hollow in the pit of his stomach. Right now, he didn't feel very fabulous. He knew he was not going to win. In fact, he thought, it was possible he might even find out how it feels to come in last. The time had come. The moment-of-truth. Time to eat dog doo.

CHAPTER THREE
EMOTIONS & THE BATTLE FOR YOUR MIND

Dan was humming as the screen door of the kitchen slammed behind him. The embarrassment he had expected to face when it was time to report his chocolate bar sales hadn't happened. No one, not even Coach Tisdale, was interested in Dan's failure. Instead, the whole team had been focused on Gabby's huge success.

Dan pulled a jug of milk from the fridge and opened the Oreo tin. He poured some milk into a cup and soaked a cookie before slopping it into his mouth. He thought about how Coach had handled the debriefing.

Since day one, Tisdale had stressed "best practices" as a way to think strategically about baseball. He seemed to be handling this chocolate bar thing the same way. Dan went over the process in his mind. Coach had asked the team members to raise their hands if they had sold at least 20 chocolate bars. Nearly everyone had raised a hand. No one seemed to notice Dan hadn't raised his. Then Coach asked for 30, and then 40. Finally, when only Gabby's hand was still in the air, he asked him to tell everyone the sales strategy he had used to sell his chocolate bars.

Gabby flashed two completed order sheets. He not only sold his chocolate bars for this week, but he had order sheets for the final two weeks of the contest, as well. He fielded questions that were peppered to him from all directions. As Gabby's strategy unfolded, Coach Tisdale called it the family-tree strategy. Gabby came from a big family, and his customers were his parents, grandparents, aunts, uncles, cousins, and even some second cousins and cousins-once-removed.

It was true that they purchased their first chocolate bar as a favor to Gabby, but when they found out how good they were, they wanted more. Coach emphasized that satisfied customers frequently become repeat customers.

As Dan took the last swallow of milk, he knew the family-tree strategy was a bust for him. It wasn't that he didn't have relatives, but they were scattered all over the world. That was great when it came to vacations, but worthless when it came to selling chocolate bars. All that aside, he was thankful Gabby's success had taken the spotlight off his failure.

Dan left the half-finished jug of milk on the counter and headed for Grant's room. He definitely needed an action plan for the week ahead. Perhaps this crazy AIDA thing could work if he found out more about the action part. Dan tapped his secret code on Grant's door.

"Yeah, wha'da'ya want?" Grant barked

"I'm ready for the war room."

Grant opened his door a couple of inches. "Yeah, well, I was ready this morning. What's with the disappearing act? I don't have all the time in the world, ya know. I'm gettin' ready for Omaha."

"I had to go. I was almost late for practice. I got to the *Talking Tree* just as the whistle blew. It was a really close call."

Grant swung the door wide open. "What an idiot. If any brother of mine is late, I'm gonna rub his nose in it."

"What do you mean, any brother? You only have one brother."

"Yeah, and if you're ever late, I won't claim ya!"

"Get off my back, it's not like robbing a bank or somethin'."

"Says who?"

"You gonna help me sell my chocolate bars or lecture me all day?"

"You've earned the lecture, stupid. Let me tell you somethin'. Only one guy has ever been late for Coach Tisdale, and he was only late once."

"Yeah, and what happened to you?"

"Very funny," Grant sneered. "It wasn't me. It was Ralph Bloomstack, before we were born. Da'ya even know who Ralph Bloomstack is?"

"Sure, he was a superstar. He was the pitcher for Dad's team when he was a student at Roosevelt. You'd have to be blind not to see his three cases of trophies outside Coach's office."

"I'm not talkin' about his bein' a superstar; I'm talkin' about the time he was late."

Dan sat down on the edge of the bed and looked expectantly. Grant loved an appreciative audience. He settled back in his chair, took a pencil from his desk, rolled it between his palms, and began. "Bloomstack was the best pitcher Roosevelt has ever seen. He was All-State three years in a row, in two sports, baseball and track. He was 'the BIG man' when Dad was in high school."

"Just like you were the big man?" Dan asked.

Grant smiled. "Appreciate the thought, but can't claim the honor." He continued, "I mean Bloomstack was really, really BIG! Coach Tisdale arrived at Roosevelt straight out of college at the beginning of Bloomstack's senior year. There wasn't much difference in their ages, really. Four or five years, at the most."

Dan tried to think what Coach Tisdale might have looked like straight out of college, but he couldn't imagine it.

"It made for an interesting scenario—Ted Tisdale, the greenhorn coach, and Ralph Bloomstack, the best-known high school athlete in the state. Some say he was the best high school pitcher that Iowa has ever seen. He was also a fantastic batter, great sprinter, and had a mind as quick as the crack of a bat. However, he wasn't much for being on time."

Dan wasn't buying it. "If he was that good, how come his name isn't in my Big League statistics book?"

"I don't know. Something happened when he went to college. Just shut up and listen. During the regional finals, Roosevelt was slated to play our archrivals, the Franklin Panthers. The entire team, except Bloomstack, was aboard the team bus. At 8:00 sharp, Coach Tisdale closed the doors, and the bus started to roll away from the curb. Just then, Bloomstack and his old man pulled into the school parking lot. Ralph ran alongside the bus, forced his hands through the rubber door guards, pulled open the bus doors, and jumped aboard. Tisdale ordered the driver to stop, and he escorted Ralph off the bus.

"Bloomstack's old man was an influential guy. He fumed and blustered, but Coach blocked the door and refused to let his star player back on that bus. The team couldn't believe what they were seein'. Nobody said 'no' to old man Bloomstack. Besides, without Ralph, the Roughriders might lose."

Dan wiggled restlessly. Grant continued. "Tisdale stood firm. Old man Bloomstack was cagey, so when bluster didn't work, he changed his strategy. He cooled down and explained it wasn't really Ralph's fault. They would have been on time if his car hadn't had a flat tire."

Grant was really getting into his story now. He stood up, and took on Coach Tisdale's mannerisms. "So, with a straight face, but a clear twinkle in his eye, Tisdale looked down his roster and said, 'I don't see *your* name here, Mr. Bloomstack, so it's okay that the flat tire made you late, but Ralph is a member of the team. He should have considered that possibility. He knows there is never a problem with being early, and ...'"

Grant paused for emphasis, and looked directly at Dan. "... he also knows there is no excuse for being late. My athletes learn that planning to be on time includes planning for the unexpected. I'm sorry, sir, but I can't cut Ralph any slack here. I'm sure he'll plan better next time.' With that Coach closed the door and the bus pulled out, leaving the two Bloomstacks standing in the parking lot."

Dan looked skeptical. "Come on, no coach is gonna kick the state's best player off the bus because he was 30 seconds late!"

Grant raised an eyebrow. "People have been tellin' that story for nearly 40 years. You gonna be the one to test it?" Grant didn't wait for an answer. He picked up his cell phone and began to dial. He motioned for Dan to leave the room. "Shove off. I have an important date tonight. Meet me in the war room tomorrow morning at ten, and we'll take up the action plan."

The next morning Dan took the steps to the war room two at a time. His foot grazed an abandoned Coke bottle at the bottom of the stairs. He struggled to keep his balance.

He was almost steady when he slid on an empty popcorn bag and went down with a thud.

"Nice slide, you're safe," Grant chuckled.

"You and your friends are a bunch of animals," Dan complained.

"Yeah, you can help me clean up when we're finished."

"Go soak your head. I'm not your janitor. I'm your client, remember?

"Right you are." Grant sat down, squared his shoulders, and straightened an imaginary tie, and started talking with a fake British accent.

"I believe we were discussing 'action', Mr. Martin. You must invite your buyer to buy. Therefore, old man, you must advertise. But before you can do that, you have to decide just who you want your advertising to influence. In short, sir, you must decide who your customers are."

"Wha'da'ya mean? Anybody who wants to buy a chocolate bar will be my customer."

Grant groaned and dropped the accent. "Focus, man. Focus is the name of the game. When I wanted you for a customer, I designed my advertising with you in mind. I was very focused. I was after one particular customer. You."

"Yeah, but I need to sell more than one chocolate bar."

Grant ignored him. "How did I reach you?"

"You A-I-D-A'd me."

"What's that mean?"

"Jeez, how short do you think my memory is?"

Grant made a fist and pounded it into the palm of his other hand. "Pow! Strike one."

"Okay, okay," Dan back peddled. "It means you got my attention, you kept my interest, you raised my desire, and you gave me the opportunity to take action."

"Good. Business is like baseball, ya gotta keep your focus."

"So I'm focused, I'm focused," Dan said. "Let's get on with the action."

"You don't want to spend a penny more on advertising than you have to. When I wanted to reach you, I didn't take an ad in a newspaper or magazine or broadcast on the radio."

"Or get a TV or Internet ad or telemarket me," Dan added.

"You're my kind of client, one who sees the big picture before he's told. Now as I was sayin', ya want to keep your advertising costs as small as possible and still reach the people most likely to buy your product. So, ya gotta decide just who your customers are."

Dan was feeling perplexed. "I already told you, anyone can buy my chocolate bars."

"It's a mistake to try and design your advertising to appeal to everybody. You need to define your target market. A lot of people in this town will buy chocolate bars today. Do you expect all of them to be your customers?"

"Of course not. Most of them don't even know what I have to sell."

"What do you have to sell?"

"What a stupid question, I've got almost three cartons of chocolate bars to sell."

"Are you sure it's chocolate bars you're selling?"

"Well, it's not peanuts and caramel corn."

"Could it be?"

"I don't know what you're getting at." Dan was getting more and more irritated.

"I'm suggesting that you have something to sell that's more appealing than chocolate bars."

"That's bad enough; I don't want anything else to sell."

"You already have something else. You just haven't recognized it." Grant drew close to Dan and lowered his voice as if what he had to say was top secret. "This is even more valuable than AIDA. You have *emotion* to sell."

"Emotion?"

"Right. Emotion is behind every decision to buy. The stronger the emotion, the more likely the sale. So 'job one' is for you to identify an emotion that will cause people to buy your chocolate bars."

"That's crazy. I buy lots of things that I'm not in love with."

"Love isn't your only emotion." Grant waited for Dan to name another emotion. When he didn't, Grant tried to draw him out by rolling his hand over and over as if they were playing charades.

"Joy?" Dan asked hesitantly.

"Yeah."

"Sadness?"

"You're on a roll."

"Fear, hate?"

"All good reasons to buy something," Grant acknowledged

"All of them?"

"Right!"

"Why would I buy something I hate?" Dan questioned.

"You might not buy something you hate, but you might buy something to avoid something you hate."

"What does that mean?"

Grant raised his eyebrows and sighed. "Name something you hate."

"I hate selling these chocolate bars."

"Good example! But it's not the selling them you hate, it's the not selling them. So when I offered you the opportunity to buy my consulting services, you jumped at the chance. I'd say you wanted to exchange your "hate" feeling for a "good" feeling."

"Yeah. So?"

"Exactly!" Grant nodded with satisfaction.

"Com'on," Dan challenged, "emotion can't be the reason for every purchase."

"Okay, Smart Saas, name a purchase with no emotion associated with it."

Dan smiled. "Gottcha! How 'bout toilet paper?"

"Hey, buddy, if you're in the bathroom and you run out of toilet paper, I bet you would feel some pretty strong emotions."

That struck Dan as very funny. He snorted and unintentionally let a loud fart. That in turn struck Grant as hilarious. Both boys were laughing, at themselves and at one another. They laughed until their sides ached.

"I'll give you one thing, Big D, you certainly illustrated my point."

Dan poked him, and they laughed some more.

Grant clapped his hands twice. "Okay, back to business here. You're right, good emotion usually does sell better than bad emotion. But, I've gotten us off track. We still haven't decided who your target market should be, or why they would buy your chocolate bars instead of someone else's."

"That's the problem. There's just too much competition. A chocolate bar is a chocolate bar; you can buy them anywhere." Dan flopped down on the floor and turned his back toward Grant.

Grant nudged Dan's behind with his foot. "Agreed, one chocolate bar is pretty much the same as the next, and there's lots of competition. But hey, without competition there is no game. When you have tough competition in the batter's box, do you just lie down and turn your back on the problem?"

"Heck no!" Dan rolled over and sat up.

"So what do you do?" Grant asked.

Dan didn't hesitate a second. "I think about the batter's stats. I get inside his mind. I think about what he is looking for, and then try to make sure he doesn't get it."

"Great! What you've been talkin' about is the 'positioning game.' To score big in the positioning game you have to get inside the other guy's mind. But, in sales your goal is to give the buyers exactly what they want, when they want it, and how they want it. Your sales pitch has to be in their strike zone, and has to have just the right spin."

"You've lost me again."

"There's this classic little book Dad gave me called *Positioning; The Battle For Your Mind*. It says we're always rankin' things in our minds. Kinda like your book on baseball statistics. We've got all these categories in our minds, and in each category we have a favorite. Our favorite baseball team, our favorite pitcher, our favorite movie, our favorite ice cream, our favorite chocolate bar, get it? We rank all sorts of things."

"That's not good news. My chocolate bars are good, but they're not my favorite."

"Don't sweat it. Your chocolate bars don't have to be the best, or the biggest. If you know your product won't rank #1, all is not lost. You just link your product to something that might rank #1 in a buyer's mind. What's your #1 reason for selling these chocolate bars?"

"To raise money for our team to go to the state tournament."

Grant nodded. "So in your mind there is a link between your chocolate bars and the state tournament. Right? Now, which one of those holds the strongest emotion for you?"

"That depends if you're talkin' love or hate."

"I repeat, which one of those holds the strongest emotion for you?"

"Are you saying I need to link my chocolate bar sales to the Roughriders going to the state tournament?"

"Right on, spoken like a true entrepreneur. I like the way you worked to reason that out. You're masterful, Dan, absolutely masterful."

Dan got up and began to march around the room playing an imaginary trumpet and blurting forth strains of *Aida*. Then he stopped in midstride. "Wait a minute. That's exactly what I've been doing all week. I told everyone I was selling the chocolate bars to send the Roughriders to the state tournament. My sales have been awful. You're the one that told me if I kept doing things the same old way, I'd keep getting the same old results."

"Well, we have to consider two things here. First, sometimes the success of a sales pitch is not in what you say, but how you say it, and ..."

"I was always real polite, even when people said 'no.'"

Grant tried to calm Dan down. "Relax, relax, it's not about polite, it's about effective, but you interrupted. I was going to say … and who you say it to. You may not have been talking to your target market." Grant picked up a stale bottle of Coke, took a long swig, and let out a loud belch.

"So where do we go from here?" Dan asked.

"How about Jimmy's, for an ice cream soda?" Grant replied.

Dan countered, "That's not what I meant."

"I knew what you meant. We'll discuss target markets over sodas. You buyin'?" Grant asked.

"No way! I'm the client. I know enough to know y*ou're* the one who's supposed to buy the drinks."

CHAPTER FOUR
SIDEWINDER

Jimmy's Cafe was jumping. Grant slowly sipped his soda. Dan concentrated on his slice of pizza, rotating it 45 degrees, and pushing the point of the triangle into his mouth as far as it would go, bit into it, and pulled the slice away. Tomato sauce painted the sides of his mouth. A string of runny cheese cascaded toward the table, then arched back up, swinging back and forth like a miniature bungee cord. With the mozzarella still dangling, he opened his mouth, exposing globs of reds and yellows, and took a large swig of his ice cream soda.

Grant turned his head and closed his eyes. "Gross."

"Yeah, it tastes better this way," Dan retorted, his voice rolling over the pizza islands that were floating in a sea of foaming ice cream soda. He finished the entire slice in six bites along with his soda, and let out a deep, rolling, satisfied belch. Grant smiled and one-upped him with a long, slow, belch of his own.

Dan wiped his mouth, first with his tongue, then his hand, and finally his sleeve. He placed his hands behind his head, stretched, and swiveled both left and right from his waist. "Okay, so tell me more about target markets."

"Okay, Sport, we've got three outstanding pieces of business on the table. Who is your target market, how do you reach them, and what do you say when you do? Agreed?"

"Yeah, but you already said my link was people who might think it was neat to help the Roughriders go to the state tournament."

"Right. So where are you gonna find those people?"

"You're the expert, you tell me."

"I'm the consultant, I ask the questions. You're supposed to come up with your own answers."

"Then you must not be asking the right questions."

Grant opened his hands and beckoned with his fingers. "Com'on, this can't be too tough. You know you're sellin' 'feel-good,' and you know you're hookin' your chocolate bars to goin' to the state tournament. Get with the program, where ya gonna find people who wanna feel good about baseball?"

"In front of their TV."

"Right, but you don't have enough dough to advertise on TV. Give me another option."

"At a ball park?"

"Sounds good to me. You got one in mind?"

"Stewart Park? Lot's of people go there."

"Stewart Park has a concession stand already."

"Yeah, but I could work the bleachers, then people wouldn't have to leave the game to go to the concession stand."

"You may have something there, Big D."

A lanky kid wearing a Yankee jersey approached their table. "Well, if it isn't the Martin brothers. We're lookin' for a couple of dudes for a pickup game; you guys want to join the opposition?"

"I'm all for opposing you, Sidewinder," Grant said, "but I'm helpin' Big D with his business plan."

"Business plan, pigeon plan, whatever. It's not frozen. It can wait. Right, Big D?"

Dan gave him a sarcastic smile. "Sure it can wait ..."

"Good, let's go," Sidewinder interrupted.

Dan finished his sentence, "... if you want to buy all my chocolate bars."

"What chocolate bars?"

"The ones I'm selling so our freshman team can go to the state tournament."

Sidewinder gloated. "Your ragtag outfit won't even win the city championship. You'd look like a bunch of clowns at state."

"You're a ssss—nake, Sidewinder. What do you know about anything?"

"I know Carlsen's pitchin' for varsity now, so what's that leave? A bunch of marshmallows, right? "

That was the type of jab Grant might give his little brother, but he wouldn't allow it from anyone else. "Dan's pitchin' for the Roughriders, Fang Face, and he's good, real good."

"Let's hope he's better at pitchin' than he is at sellin' chocolate bars."

Grant stood and faced off Sidewinder. "He's not bad, considering he's just sold you five of them."

"You don't look like a mongoose to me."

Grant stepped inside Sidewinder's bubble. "Looks can be deceiving. Cough up your fiver."

Sidewinder stepped back. "What am I gonna do with five crummy chocolate bars?"

Jimmy, the owner of the cafe, caught the action out of the corner of his eye. He was at their booth with the speed of a wireless hookup. He stretched his 5-foot-6 frame and reached high to put his arm around Sidewinder's shoulder. "How's it going, Sidewinder?"

"Fine, until these two bullies tried to extort five bucks out of me for some stale chocolate bars."

"That right, boys? You bullying this poor little kid here?" Jimmy bent at the waist to exaggerate Sidewinder's 6-foot-3 height.

Grant shrugged. "Let's just say he's payin' a fine for slandering Dan's pitching skills."

Jimmy smiled at Dan. "Selling chocolate bars, are you? How are your sales going?" Jimmy was genuinely interested.

"Not great. I'm thinking of selling them at Stewart Park though, and then sales ought to pick up."

Jimmy looked surprised. "Ralph Bloomstack gave you permission to sell chocolate bars at Stewart Park?"

Sidewinder hissed, "Maaaa...n, I've worked for Bloomstack; he'll eat you alive and use your bones for toothpicks."

"You're full of it, Sidewinder," Dan glared.

"He's full of it alright," Jimmy agreed, "but Bloomstack is a tough negotiator, fair-minded though. His word is as good as gold, *if* you can get it."

"Don't sweat it, Big D," Grant reassured Dan. "I'll give you another one of Dad's little books called *Getting to Yes*. It's a quick read. You can read it tonight instead of being a couch potato. It's pretty neat. It'll help you negotiate all kinds of stuff. Even help you with the girls."

Sidewinder looked across at the pretty girl behind the counter. "That right? I'd like to borrow that book."

"You can borrow it, but who's gonna read it to you?" Grant taunted.

"Shove it, Turdhead. You guys gonna play ball, or just sit here worryin' about old man Bloomstack? Let's go, maybe you can talk some of the guys into buying your chocolate bars."

"I don't have'em with me."

"You just bring the guys over here when you finish your game, and I'll advance you all the chocolate bars you need," Jimmy offered.

"You'd really lend me some chocolate bars?"

"Sure, we businessmen stick together. Friendly competition and all that. Who knows, your customers may decide to buy one of my hamburgers to go along with one of your chocolate bars."

Using his baseball mitt as a gavel, Sidewinder slammed it on the table. "Meeting's adjourned. Let's play ball."

And play ball they did. It was a terrific afternoon on the sandlot for the Martin brothers. Grant was particularly satisfied that his last pick-up game before heading off to Omaha was with Dan, and that Dan had managed to strike out Sidewinder twice.

Before the game started Dan had created a win-win situation for himself when he talked everyone into agreeing that the loosing side would buy chocolate bars for the winning side. The frosting on the cake came, however, when Sidewinder slapped five ones down on the table in front of Dan. "Ya earned them, man; I gotta respect your pitchin'."

Dan smiled. "Thanks." He slipped the five ones into his pocket, and handed Sidewinder the last five chocolate bars from the inventory that Jimmy had lent him.

"I'll tell ya what. Since Grant is gonna be girl watchin' in Omaha for the summer, anytime you need a big brother to pitch to, just give me a holler; I'll catch a few for ya."

"Really? Gabby goes on vacation in a couple of weeks. I'll give you a call."

"Sounds good! Who knows, I might just be catchin' for a future Hall of Fame superstar." He shoved four of the chocolate bars into his jacket pocket, opened the fifth, and dropped the wrapper on the floor.

"Up and out, Sidewinder," Jimmy called from behind the counter.

Sidewinder bent and picked up the paper. "Ya don't miss a thing, do ya, Old Man?" He smiled, crushed the papers into a ball, and tossed it to Jimmy as he went out the door.

Dan turned to Grant. "I can't figure him out. One minute he's rotten, and the next he's nice, and then before you can blink, he's rotten again."

Grant shrugged. "Some of the guys think he just wants attention and hasn't figured out a good way to get it. He's not stupid; someday he may wise up."

"Ya think?"

Grant pushed his chair back. "I have to pick up Linda Rae; you want a ride to the varsity game?"

"Nope, I'll take my bike; I'm meeting the guys."

CHAPTER FIVE
GOOD, REAL GOOD!

The speed of Gabby's chatter accelerated as the situation on the field intensified. His motor mouth was showing no sign of running out of gas. "Way to go Carlsen." "You're the man." "Razzle him." "Dazzle him." "This is the one."

Chandler and Spider couldn't match Gabby's chatter in speed, but they made up for that with volume. Dan, in contrast, sat on the edge of his seat in absolute silence, his eyes darting between the pitcher's mound and home plate.

Gabby nudged Spider and nodded toward Dan. They shared a knowing smile. They knew he was in the moment, imagining himself on the mound, and feeling the pressure of facing the batter with a full count at the bottom of the ninth. The foursome had a perfect vantage point from the bleachers directly above the Roosevelt Roughriders' dugout.

"Can you believe this? Varsity is gonna get a shutout their first game of the season!" Chandler's voice was filled with both admiration and surprise.

"Don't jinks us man, it's not a done deal," Dan snapped.

Chandler jerked back, more amused than offended.

Dan watched every detail of Bob Carlsen's pitching, so calm, cool, and confident. He sure didn't show any signs of feeling the pressure. Regardless of their conversation at practice yesterday, nothing seemed to knock Carlsen off stride. Dan wanted to be like that, but he hadn't quite learned how to master his tension in tight situations. A batter with a full count was nothing new for him. He taught himself to face down that situation in junior high, but a shutout, that was something else. A shutout was still a dream for Dan.

"Wha'da'ya'wanna bet Carlsen will do it?" Gabby asked.

Dan's response was quick and sharp. "Shut up and watch the game."

Gabby laughed and turned his attention to the field, but he didn't shut up. "Break that Panther." "Steal his roar." "Send him an express, big guy." "Go for it man; he's waiting you out."

"No! He's not!" Dan corrected. "Check out how the guy's holding his bat, look at his stance. He's either gonna wallop the ball, or go down tryin'. Look at his front shoulder, it's dropped, he's wantin' a high ball."

"Where did you get your crystal ball?" Gabby sneered.

Dan didn't answer. He was nearly motionless except for his rapid breathing, and his right thumb was nervously massaging the palm of his left hand. He felt a trickle of sweat between his shoulder blades. Shifting his attention from the batter to Carlsen, he studied every detail of his delivery: the placement of his feet, the rise and fall of his arms, the rock of his body, his extension, his balance, the push of his legs, and finally the catapult of the ball, low and inside. Dan smiled as the Panther batter corkscrewed to the ground. "I read him right," he whispered to himself.

"Strike three!" The umpire bellowed as he jabbed three fingers into the air and swirled around twice, creating a small dust cloud at his feet. The crowd erupted in a thunderclap. Winning cheers and losing groans filled the air. Dan jumped up, extending his arms in a "V." A wild victorious scream carried away his pent-up tension. The varsity team members raised Carlsen to their shoulders, circled the bases, and headed for their bus.

The Fabulous Four jostled their way down the bleachers and zigzagged through the crowd to where the team bus was loading. Several other members from the freshman team saw Dan and gravitated toward him. They all identified with what had just happened on the field, saying things like, "We're next," and "Our turn's coming." Dan began to feel the burden of expectations, but he managed to smile and high-five his way through the situation. When the crowd broke up, Chandler, who was naturally empathetic, noticed Dan's relief.

On the way back to their bikes, the boys walked four abreast, in their fabulous four formation. Chandler, who frequently slouched to minimize his 6-foot-2 frame, was walking tall, his shoulders square and his chin up. His smile, which was always handsome, seemed brighter than usual against his dark skin. He easily could have been mistaken as the oldest of the group, but he was actually the youngest. In the last few months, he had shot up like Iowa corn in July. Gabby joked he could almost hear him grow. Surprisingly, in spite of his spurt, Chandler was not awkward. He never lost his speed or coordination, or his ability to channel a baseball with precise accuracy from center field to anywhere in the infield.

Dan 'Big D' Martin came next. He had been the tallest of the boys in junior high, but Chandler had changed all that, at least temporarily. Dan willingly gave up his lead position in their walking formation, but there was no question that he was still the leader. He worked hard at building a powerhouse brain under his curly red hair, and the guys respected that. An outsider probably wouldn't guess his importance in the group. He was a quiet leader who led by example.

After his dad was killed in the Middle East, Dan became a whole lot quieter. Sometimes his friends worried about him, but not tonight. It was clear his mind was on baseball. As they walked, Dan occasionally stopped, wound up, and pitched an imaginary ball across an imaginary home plate.

"Strike three," yelled Spider, and twirled to imitate the umpire's last call.

Dan smiled. "Was Carlsen spectacular or what?"

"Man, his pitchin' was something else again," Spider agreed.

"Com'on, he didn't do it alone. There was a championship team behind him," Chandler reminded them.

Gabby nodded. "Yeah, but even so, he was pure beauty in motion, if I ever saw it."

Chandler agreed. "I'll give ya that. The man has power. I'd love to have power like that!"

Dan added, "More important, he has control. Heck, I have power, but sometimes I'm in trouble if I have to put somethin' on the ball."

Chandler gave him a gentle shoulder block. "Hey man, you're doin' okay. Don't forget, we're always there to back you up."

"We're the best!" said Gabby, as he quick-stepped from his position on the inside of the line to strut out in front. "We're GOOD! REAL GOOD!"

"Good for what?" Spider shoved Gabby playfully from behind, and then made a quick get-away. Patrick "Gabby" Sullivan had the perfect build for a catcher. His frame was built close to the ground, and he had mega core-body strength. Gabby's baby face and big dimples reflected his natural good humor, but they could also be deceptive. If he got angry, look out. He was not someone to be on the wrong side of. But, tonight Gabby just laughed, and got back in formation.

Miguel "Spider" Hernandez, seeing he was in no danger, did a couple of somersaults and ended up in his spot between Dan and Gabby. Spider was, without question, the quickest and most agile member of the group. Actually, he was the most outstanding gymnast in the city, and could be a state contender, but baseball was the only sport that interested him.

His family was from Cuba, and baseball was in his blood. Spider's dad once showed the guys a bat and ball he made as a kid so he could play the game. The baseball was a stone wrapped in rags, and the bat had been carved from a tree branch.

When it came to baseball, Spider had focus. He never took his big black laser-beam eyes off the ball. If it came anywhere near him, the ball was captured in the web of his glove. Unless he fouled up off the field, the shortstop position he coveted on the freshman team would definitely be his.

When they reached their bikes, Gabby asked, "So, wha'da'ya'wanna do? How 'bout stoppin' by Jimmy's?"

"Count me out, I'm in training," Dan said as he pushed off for a running mount.

"Com'on, just an hour or so, you'll still get eight straight. We gotta celebrate Carlsen's shutout," Gabby called after him.

Chandler casually draped his long leg across his bike. "Like I keep tellin' ya, it was the team's shutout. Carlsen didn't do it alone."

"Ya comin' to Jimmy's?" Gabby asked.

"I'm with 'Big D'; see you at practice tomorrow."

Spider wrapped his arm around Gabby's shoulder. "I'll go with you buddy, if you agree we only stay long enough to congratulate the varsity team. No food. No drinks."

"Are you kidding? I'm gonna party. Jimmy's will be jumpin'. You can't pass that up."

"I can, but it's your choice. Just make sure you're at the top of your game at practice tomorrow, or you'll be warmin' the bench on our first game."

"Don't worry about me. I'm always in front of the competition. Which reminds me, how you doin' with your sales?"

Spider circled around Gabby without touching his hands to the handle bars. "You'll find out tomorrow," he said before heading his separate way.

Gabby, always determined to have the last word, called over his shoulder. "I'm gonna win the contest, I'm GOOD, REAL GOOD!"

CHAPTER SIX
WARMING THE BENCH

Dan viewed himself in the full-length mirror and smiled. His new uniform looked sharp. He grabbed his glove, slid down the banister, and headed out the kitchen door. It hadn't slammed before he realized he had forgotten to look at his pre-game checklist. He glanced at his watch, turned, and took the stairs two at a time. Opening his closet door, he ran his finger down the checklist. He had forgotten the handkerchief he would need if his hands got sweaty. He took one from his dresser, tucked it in his rear pocket, and admired himself in the mirror one last time before heading out.

He had been looking forward to this freshman opener for months, yet today he found his excitement was mingled with a deep sadness. This would be his first school game without his dad being in the stands cheering for him. It was times like this that Dan missed his father the most. He felt a tear forming, and tried to hold it back. He couldn't. Swerving his bike off the path, he headed toward a clump of trees. Dan parked his bike and ran into the woods, tears running down his cheeks. He dropped to the ground, muffled his mouth in his hands, and cried until his eyes burned. Slowly he gained control of his emotions, took several deep breaths, pulled his handkerchief from his pocket, and dried his tears.

When Dan walked out of the clump of trees, the sun warmed his face. It felt good. He looked at his reflection in his bicycle mirror. Anyone could see he had been crying. He looked around. There was no one in sight. He biked to the drinking fountain near Diamond 3, took four long swigs of water, and splashed his face. He closed his eyes and let the arching water massage them. He looked again into his handlebar mirror. He looked much better. The whites of his eyes were still red, but his skin was no longer blotchy. He remounted and headed for Diamond 1. He had done everything on his pre-game checklist, but he didn't feel ready to play. He was emotionally drained. His heart wasn't in it.

Gabby noticed Dan arrive. "Heads up," he yelled as he threw him a ball. Dan caught it and joined Gabby along the third base line to warm up. Gabby was his usual chattering self. Dan felt relief that Gabby hadn't noticed he had been crying. They had just started getting into the rhythm of the warm-up when Coach Tisdale approached. "Gabby, I'd like you to switch with Buzz Wilkie for this warm-up."

"Sure Coach, right away." Gabby was clearly surprised. He shrugged a questioning shoulder to Dan and trotted off to catch for Ken Page. Judging from their reactions, Ken and Buzz were also surprised.

Dan wondered what was up. He knew Ken was strong competition for the mound. Had Coach noticed that he was not totally focused? Was Ken going to be the starting pitcher this season? Dan respected Ken Page as a pitcher. They had both been training hard. However, Dan thought he had won the competition when Coach assigned Bob Carlsen to coach him. Now he realized it might have been because Coach thought Dan was the one who needed the most help.

Gabby really didn't have competition for his catcher's position. The guys would razz Gabby for saying, "I'm the best; I'm good, real good," but it was the truth. He was good, real good.

Dan tried to concentrate on pitching to Buzz, but things just weren't clicking. Buzz was getting his signals mixed up and fumbling the ball. Dan almost said something; then it occurred to him that things hadn't been going well for him today. Maybe he was the one who was mixed up.

"Hey, Big D, show them what you got." Dan turned to see Grant standing on the sidelines, and walked toward him. "Looks like I'm not going to start."

"Why do you say that?"

"Coach has Gabby catching for Ken Page."

"Yeah, well, you don't have to just hand it to him. Maybe Coach is seeing how you work under pressure."

"I'm really missing Dad. This is the first game ever, that he's not been here."

"Yeah, I know, I miss him, too. When I get really down, I try to think about what Dad would do. Sometimes I imagine him coming into my room and sitting down to talk things over with me." Grant paused. "I figure if he was talking to you right now, he'd tell you it's okay to re-member him in your quiet times, but right now, it's time to concentrate on the game. To get out there and do the best you can do."

"That sounds good, but it's not that easy." Dan felt an-other tear forming.

Grant took Dan by the shoulders and gently whispered, "Dad is always with you. He's in your mind, and in your heart. Use your imagination. If you let him, he can be with you and coach you in this game. You can honor him by being the best you can be. Remember he always said, 'When you play your best, there are no regrets.' If he were here today, you know he would be expecting you to give it your all. If it helps, just imagine him sitting next to me in the bleachers."

Dan didn't say anything. He just smiled a weak smile and went back to his warm-up. Slowly, very slowly, his focus and energy began to return. He and Buzz began to connect. By the time Coach called them to the dugout, Dan was back to normal. He didn't hover around Coach waiting to be posted. He was sure Ken Page would be the starting pitcher, since Gabby had been warming up with him.

Dan knew he had done his best. He felt comfortable with himself as he took his usual seat in the center of the bench. He was a little surprised to discover he didn't feel any jealousy toward Ken Page. He realized Ken was a tough, and fair, competitor. Coach had made a decision. That was that. Dan knew he would keep trying. Perhaps he would start the next game.

However, that was not the way it was to be. When Coach called the lineup, it was Gabby who was on the bench. As Dan ran toward the mound, he heard Gabby, who could never seem to hold his tongue, ask, "Hey, Coach, how come I'm not starting?"

Coach responded, "Give it a little thought, I think you can come up with the answer."

Dan grinned a toothy grin. He remembered how his dad used those same words.

In the first inning, Wilson grabbed a two-run lead. There was a runner on second when a weak hitter got lucky. He was late on his swing, but still managed a line drive just inside the first base line. It got past the first baseman, but Roosevelt's right fielder ran it down and fired it home in an attempt to out the base runner. Buzz caught the ball, but when the runner slid into home feet first, Buzz instinctively jumped back. Then he immediately corrected, and tagged the guy. It only took him a second to correct his action, but that's all the runner needed.

Buzz had the good sense to fire the ball to third in an attempt to cut off the fellow who had hit the line drive, but he was rattled and his throw went above the third baseman's reach. Spider had anticipated a throw to third, and had moved from his shortstop position to back up third base. The batter rounded third and headed for home. Spider snatched the ball and fired it home, Buzz, to his credit, held his ground. The runner headed back to third. Buzz got his arm under control and his throw to third was perfect. They had the runner trapped and they started to close in, but Buzz just didn't have the experience, and the runner got around him and scored the second run.

Dan knew just how lucky that batter had been. For the past two weeks he had been spying on the Wilson freshman team from under a bush on the hillside overlooking their practice diamond. He felt he had a good handle on the batting strength of his opponents, and that batter's timing was consistently slow.

"Everybody gets lucky sometimes," he could hear his father's words in his mind. "Let it go, focus, and get on with the game."

He stepped off the mound and motioned for Buzz to join him. When they came together, Dan put his arm around Buzz's shoulder. He ignored the errors Buzz had made, but shared his dad's wisdom. "That guy got lucky; that happens sometimes. We have to let it go. If we focus, we can hold them down. Are you with me?"

Buzz nodded. "I'm with you. Focus, focus, focus."

The two walked back to their positions. Buzz squatted down, smiled, and then exaggerated a silent "focus" with his mouth. Dan was definitely focused. To his credit, Buzz was able to do the same.

When Dan returned to the dugout in the bottom of the first, Gabby was on the left end of the bench, as far from Coach Tisdale as he could get. He was in a mope. Dan sat in his usual spot in the center of the bench, but it felt funny. He was used to having Gabby on his left. He got up, walked down to the end of the bench and gave Gabby a nudge. "Move over, give me some room." Gabby scooted over.

"What's the deal? How come you're benched?"

Gabby nodded toward Coach Tisdale. "Ask him."

"I'm not askin' him!"

Gabby just shrugged.

Dan nudged him again. "It's not the same out there without you. I can't hear your chatter."

"I'm not chatterin'."

"Wha'da'ya mean, you're not chatterin'? You're still part of this team, even if you are on the bench."

"Yeah, well, you're not on the bench. So how would you know?"

"You shouldn't be on the bench either, so why are you?"

"Shut up, I don't want to hear it."

"Yeah, well, I want to hear from you. You should either be supporting this team or get out of the uniform."

"Shove it!" Gabby exploded, pushing Dan off the end of the bench and left the dug out.

Dan winced as his right shoulder hit the ground. It might have brought tears to his eyes if he hadn't been all cried out already. He got to his feet and started after Gabby, who was now leaning against the fence with his back to the game.

Chandler, who was observing, stepped between them. "You're on deck, Big D," he said. Dan walked to the deck and selected a bat. He rubbed his right shoulder as he watched Spider hit a high fly to left field for the second out.

As Dan approached the batter's box, he heard Gabby's chatter. Normally he would have been pleased with Gabby's change of heart, but not now. The push had caught him off guard, and he wasn't sure how bad his shoulder was hurt. Fortunately, Dan was a switch-hitter. He decided to favor his right shoulder and bat left-handed. Even so, the pain affected his swing, and he struck out.

Dan threw the bat toward the deck, and headed toward the mound. After only a couple of warm-up throws, Coach Tisdale was on the field. "It looks like you're having some trouble out here."

"There's a little pain in my right shoulder, Coach."

Tisdale put his hand on Dan's shoulder. Dan winced. "You'll have to sit out the rest of this game. Then we'll see what Doc has to say." Coach Tisdale signaled for Ken Page.

Dan was extremely disappointed as he walked back to the dugout, and took his usual place near the center of the bench.

"Hey, Big D, anything I can do?" Grant was leaning over the fence at the end of the dugout.

"Naw, sore shoulder, Coach will take me to see Doc after the game."

"D'ya want me to come along?"

"I'll see you at home after, okay?"

"You're sure?" Grant clearly wanted to go with Dan, but he didn't want to force the situation.

"I'm sure." Dan turned to watch the action on the field.

Both teams played well the remainder of the game. Roosevelt held Wilson to the initial two runs, but lost the game. As the team gathered their gear, Gabby grumbled, "Tisdale lost this game. He should have had me behind home plate. They would have never gotten those runs in the first inning if I had been playing."

Chandler looked disgusted. "Hey, you only need to look into a mirror to see the villain, and it's not Coach. We all know why you were on the bench. You need to face the truth."

Dan looked surprised. "Somethin' goin' on I don't know about?"

Spider halfway whispered, "He's been breaking training regular like."

Chandler's voice was far from a whisper. "Partying every chance he gets. Thinks that makes him a big shot." He got into Gabby's bubble and glared at him. "I want nothing to do with you until you get back into training." Then he turned to the others. "Let's get out of here; this guy makes me sick."

"You guys go on,' Dan said, "I need to talk with Gabby."

Chandler shrugged, "Suit yourself, but I wouldn't waste my time with him. He only thinks of himself. Come on Spider, let's go."

Dan turned to Gabby. "Is what they're saying true? Have you been breaking training? Is that why you were benched?"

"Yeah, could be."

"Could be?"

"Okay, I've taken in a few parties lately. What are people so upset about? I'm still the best catcher in the league, and we wouldn't have lost if I had been playin'."

"We might not have lost if I had been playing either." Dan knew that wasn't true. Ken Page hadn't allowed any runs, but he wanted a comeback, and that was the first one that had popped into his head.

"Well, it's not my fault you were pitching lousy," Gabby said in a righteous tone.

"That's exactly whose fault it is. I wouldn't have hurt my shoulder if you hadn't pushed me off the bench."

Gabby's eyes widened. For once he seemed to be without words. When he looked at Dan there was deep concern in his eyes. He slowly melted to the ground and stared out into space. Dan sat down next to him.

"Man, you're my best friend. I'd never hurt you on purpose," Gabby's voice cracked. "I've been stupid. Chandler's right. This whole thing is my fault. I was tryin' to be a big shot, hangin' out with the older guys. They never respected me, just treated me like I was a favorite puppy or somethin'."

"So, you gonna get back into training then?"

"I've lost the team's respect, too. You're the only one speakin' to me."

Dan waited to make sure Gabby had finished his thought, and then he said, "The big question is, do you respect yourself?"

Gabby shook his head.

"Then maybe you need to decide what you have to do to earn back respect, especially your own."

The boys hadn't noticed Coach Tisdale approach them. Dan wondered how long he had been standing behind them, and what he might have overheard. Coach looked down at them. "The gear's packed. Doc said to drop by his house, and he will have a look at that shoulder of yours."

"Can I come, too?" Gabby asked.

"May I come, too?" Coach corrected. "The answer is yes."

As they walked toward the car, Gabby hesitated. "Coach, I've done some pretty stupid things lately."

Coach smiled. "Recognizing you have a problem is the first step. Does that mean you'll keep your training schedule, and give the team one hundred percent?"

"Yes, sir!"

"That's good. I expect my players to discipline themselves so no one else has to."

Gabby felt a surge of guilt redden his ears. "Yes, sir. I understand."

"Hmm," was all Coach replied. They rode to the doctor's office in silence.

CHAPTER SEVEN
TWISTER

When Dan got home from visiting the doctor, he shut himself in his bedroom and curled up with the two books that had been his dad's. He opened *Getting to Yes* and found an inscription from Roger Fisher. Dan had thought he was all cried out, but the tears started again. He missed his dad terribly. He grabbed a pillow to bury his sobs. He didn't want to burden Mom or Grant with his sorrow; they had enough of their own. When the tears stopped, his eyes burned too much to read. He fell asleep hugging the books to his chest.

He awoke at 4 in the morning to find himself covered with a light blanket. In the moonlight he saw his dad's books were on his side table. Someone, probably Mom, had put his shoes and socks on the floor. He turned on his bedside light, and began reading *Getting to Yes.*

Dan found the book full of surprises. He had always believed that if he won, the other guy had to lose. He had a hard time getting his mind around the idea that both sides should win in a successful negotiation. He had never played a game where both sides won. Another thing that was weird in the book was the idea that he should help the other side get what they needed. That just didn't compute. Why should he help his opponent?

Then with a sudden awareness, he found himself in tears again. If countries negotiated better, instead of going to war, perhaps his dad wouldn't have been killed in the Middle East. In that instant, he decided he would work as hard at being a good negotiator as he did at being a good pitcher.

Dan wasn't understanding everything that was in his dad's little book, but he knew he was getting the big ideas. He didn't believe he had to sweat the details right now, because he figured Mr. Bloomstack would jump at the chance to help the Roughriders go to the state tournament. After all, the guy was a former state champion, and Roosevelt was his alma mater.

He had never met Ralph Bloomstack, but he knew he had a reputation of being a no-nonsense kind of guy, who held himself, and those around him, to a high standard, just like Coach Tisdale. Grant said Mr. Bloomstack was a good businessman. Jimmy said Mr. Bloomstack was a tough negotiator, but fair—a man of his word, *if* you could get it. Dan didn't put any stock in Sidewinder calling him "Old Blow-his-stack." Sidewinder probably got fired because he was too lazy or sloppy to meet Mr. Bloomstack's standard.

Dan found *Getting to Yes* was a quick read, just like Grant had said. He finished it before breakfast, then showered, combed his hair, and dressed in his favorite jeans and Roughriders tee. He intended to make a good first impression with Mr. Bloomstack.

As backup insurance he stuffed *Getting to Yes* and his notes into the saddlebag of his bike. He figured that was a little like having a relief pitcher in the bullpen.

When he arrived at the concession stand, the windows were still shuttered. He went around back. Looking through the screen door, he could see a storeroom. "Anyone here?" he called.

A cheerful, "The door's open," came in reply.

"Are you Mr. Bloomstack?" Dan asked.

"Who's asking?"

"I'm Dan Martin, Mr. Bloomstack. I'd like to talk with you about selling chocolate bars at the games for the next two weeks."

"Sorry, Mr. Dan Martin, I have all the help I need."

"Oh, I don't want a job, Mr. Bloomstack."

"I thought you said you wanted to sell chocolate bars."

"I do. I wanna sell them to raise money for our team to go to the state tournament."

Mr. Bloomstack raised an eyebrow. "Let me get this straight, Mr. Dan Martin. You want me to give you permission to sell *your* chocolate bars, at *my* park, to raise money for *your* baseball team, to go to the state tournament?"

"Right."

"Just like that. You walk in my back door and announce you want to take over my territory."

"Oh, nothin' like that. I just wanna sell chocolate bars for two weeks. That's how much longer our team contest lasts."

"Look there, over your right shoulder. Wha'da'ya see there on that second shelf? I've got chocolate bars of my own to sell. If my crowd buys your chocolate bars, who's gonna buy my chocolate bars? Sounds like a territory hustle to me."

Mr. Bloomstack bent over until his face was only a foot or so from Dan. "I understand why you want to sell your chocolate bars in my ballpark, Mr. Dan Martin, but I don't see why I should say yes. I run a concession stand here, not a charity."

Dan looked down at his shoes, feeling he had made a fool of himself. "I'm sorry, Mr. Bloomstack, I didn't mean any disrespect."

Bloomstack straightened. "Okay, kid, none taken. You better run along now, I've got work to do."

Dan rushed out of the concession stand, jumped on his bike, and peddled away as fast as he could. He took a shortcut across the outfield of Diamond 1. The grass was wet from a recent rain. His bike did an unexpected wheelie, and Dan hit the ground hard. Blood oozed from his left elbow. His pants were grass-stained and his favorite shirt ripped. He felt his right shoulder; it was no worse.

Anyone could see he was a mess on the outside, but he felt more of a mess on the inside. Mr. Bloomstack had torn through his ego like a giant twister. Maybe Sidewinder was right about old Blow-his-stack.

Dan was really feeling sorry for himself. He had felt so sure. How could he face Grant? He dreaded seeing Sidewinder and hearing his gleeful hissing. This wasn't the way it was supposed to turn out.

He felt like throwing up. He turned on his side and pulled his knees up to his chest, closed his eyes, and took several deep breaths. That eased the nausea. He rolled over on his back and just lay there for several minutes watching little puffballs of cumulus clouds drift by. He thought a dark, wild tornado would be more appropriate. He really hated Bloomstack. Blow-his-stack, maniac, thunder crack, mean attack, kick him back, Bloomstack, whack, whack, whack. Bloomstack, whack, whack, whack. He stomped his feet with each whack, and then he began to laugh.

The second he laughed, he thought about one of the points in *Getting to Yes*. A new mantra started up in his mind. "Separate the people from the problem, separate the people from the problem, separate ..." Taking a deep breath, Dan sat up and looked over at the concession stand.

Clearly, he didn't get it right the first time. He had struck out in his dealings with Mr. Bloomstack. If at first you don't succeed …. He pulled himself off the grass and righted his bike. He examined it closely for damage. The bike was in better shape than he was.

He was ready to try again, but what was he going to say? He opened his saddlebag and took out his notes. *What does the other side care about?* Dan had guessed wrong. He thought Mr. Bloomstack would care about the Rough-riders and the state tournament, but it was clear that wasn't his first priority.

Dan now realized that no matter how important selling chocolate bars was to him, or how important it was to his team, it didn't seem to matter to Mr. Bloomstack. That was the reality. Bloomstack had all the power in this negotia-tion, and all he seemed to care about was not losing money.

Dan needed a different angle to approach old Blow-his-stack. OOPS! He realized he wasn't separating the people from the problem. He'd have to start thinking of Mr. Bloomstack in a new way, a friendlier way. Maybe he'd call him Mr. B. That sounded a whole lot friendlier. But, before he could call him anything, he knew he had to fol-low the advice in *Getting To Yes,* and think of a win-win strategy that wouldn't take money out of Mr. Bloom-stack's pocket.

CHAPTER EIGHT
IF AT FIRST …

Dan felt confident. There was a wide smile on his face and a bounce in his step as he approached the concession stand a second time. He gave a rhythmic knock on the screen door.

Mr. Bloomstack looked up. "Good grief, would you look at what the cat drug in. What do you want this time, boy?"

Dan stepped inside. "I was just thinking, Mr. Bloomstack. You don't have a concession stand at the outlying diamonds. So, if I sold my chocolate bars there, I wouldn't be takin' any money out of your pocket, right?"

Mr. Bloomstack looked amused. He turned to a lady cutting buns at a table on the opposite side of the room. "Would you believe this kid, Sally? First, he wants to peddle his chocolate bars right here under my nose, and now he wants to set up competition with me on the outlying diamonds."

She put her knife down, covered the buns with a large white cloth, and smiled as she approached Dan. "What's your name, son?"

"Dan Martin, ma'am."

"I'm Sally Bloomstack. Why are you interested in selling chocolate bars?"

"I'm tryin' to raise money for our team to go to the state tournament."

"State tournament, eh? That's a worthy goal," she said encouragingly.

Mr. Bloomstack objected. "Yeah, well, protecting my investment is a worthy goal, too."

A large wall clock chimed 5 o'clock. "Time to raise the shutters, Sally," Mr. Bloomstack said as he put his hand on Dan's shoulder and walked him toward the door. "I admire your persistence, Mr. Dan Martin, but we've got to get to work now."

"Good luck, Dan," Mrs. Bloomstack called after him, "perhaps you can sell your chocolate bars at Logan Park. There's no concession stand there."

Dan thought to himself, Logan Park sucks, its clear across town. The only time there's a crowd there is on Saturday mornings when little kids play T-ball. Instead, he smiled and said, "I'll stop back when you're less busy, Mr. B."

"I'm always busy," Mr. Bloomstack called after him.

Dan felt almost glad that the clock chimed before he had received a definitive "No." This gave him time to consider how to better his offer. As he peddled toward the grove of trees just beyond center field, he considered Mrs. Bloomstack's suggestion. Logan Park wasn't the best, but it could work as his second best option. He tried to remember what the book *Getting to Yes* had called that. He thought it was something like BATNA, but he wasn't positive. He couldn't remember what the acronym stood for. He leaned his bike against a tree and rummaged in his saddlebag looking for his notes.

The inside of his bag was a mess. In his rush to get to the concession stand, he hadn't closed the wrapper on his chocolate bar. Melted chocolate was on everything. He pulled out his notes, swiped at the globs of chocolate with his finger, and then licked his finger clean. The paper was still smudged, so he put it to his mouth and licked the remaining warm sweetness from the paper until it was readable.

He was right about BATNA. That made him feel good. It stood for "**B**est **A**lternative **T**o a **N**egotiated **A**greement." He studied it, committing it to memory. He had written down two points under BATNA. The first said: Your BATNA should be the standard against which to measure everything that the other side offers you. The second said: Any offer you make should be better than your BATNA, otherwise you're not gaining anything.

Logan Park was a pretty good BATNA. The more he thought about it, the better it looked. In fact, it started looking so good he figured he might work the T-ball games on Saturday mornings as an extra business on the side, but he still needed to succeed with the Bloomstack deal.

Dan wasn't going to put the notes back into his messy saddlebag, so he shoved them into his jeans pocket and stepped into the clearing at the edge of center field. It was the perfect spot for shagging balls. Other kids might come to challenge his territory, but for now, he was king. He could shift easily toward either left or right field. Stewart umpires would pay a buck for every ball returned, so being behind center field offered good opportunity. It also gave him a neat vantage point for watching the game.

As the stands began to fill, so did the shagging field. Both pitchers were in top form. They allowed very few hits, and none beyond the infield. With no action coming his way, he had plenty of time to consider how to sweeten his offer to Mr. Bloomstack.

Dan had pitched what he thought were some pretty good business opportunities, but Mr. Bloomstack obviously didn't consider them in his strike zone. As Dan thought about it, he realized that both offers he had pitched were in favor of himself and his team.

Dan had to admit he hadn't really put himself into the other side's shoes, as *Getting to Yes* had advised. He hadn't asked what was good for Mr. Bloomstack. What did Mr. Bloomstack need to make a deal? He now knew that Mr. Bloomstack thought both of Dan's offers would take money out of his pocket. If Dan wanted a deal, he had better think of a way to put money *into* Mr. Bloomstack's pocket.

During the bottom of the sixth inning, a new idea occurred to Dan. The score was 0-0 with one out and two men on base. Spectators were glued to their seats. Dan was confident that no one would take their eyes off the game to buy a snack. He ran along the sidelines and straight to the concession stand. He was right. Not a soul in sight.

Mr. Bloomstack saw him coming. "Well, Mr. Dan Martin, are you here to try to pick my pocket again, or do you intend to put some money in it?"

"Ralph," his wife admonished.

"I'd like a hot dog and a Coke, Mr. B," Dan responded cheerily.

"That's more like it," responded Mr. Bloomstack in kind.

The Bloomstacks were a well-practiced team. Mrs. Bloomstack prepared the hot dog, while Mr. Bloomstack drew the drink. They placed his order before him in unison. Dan paid for his purchase, but stayed right at the counter to eat it.

"You're a ball player, are you?" asked Mr. Bloomstack.

"Uh, huh."

"What position do you play?"

"Pitch mostly."

"A pitcher, huh?"

"Yup," Dan said, his mouth full of hot dog.

"You're pretty good, are ya?"

"I'm part of a pretty good team."

"Uh, huh," Mr. Bloomstack acknowledged.

Then Dan decided to grab control of the conversation. "You still play ball, Mr. B.?"

"Do I look like a ball player?" Mr. Bloomstack grabbed a towel, gave the counter a swipe, and threw the towel into the sink.

"He was a champion pitcher in his day," volunteered Mrs. Bloomstack.

"Yeah, I know, I've seen pictures in the trophy cases at school, and Coach Tisdale says he was the best pitcher Stewart has ever seen."

Mr. Bloomstack grunted, moved toward the rear of the concession stand and began to shuffle cartons around.

Mrs. Bloomstack moved close to Dan and said softly, "Pay him no mind, Dan, he loves baseball. He'll talk baseball with you all day long. He just doesn't want to think about his own baseball career. He lost a lot of big dreams when his career was cut short."

"What happened?" Dan whispered.

Mrs. Bloomstack continued to wipe the already clean counter. Dan thought she was trying to decide if she should tell him. Finally, she leaned close and in a confidential voice said, "Ralph has always been big on long-term strategy. So in his final year of high school he decided to go to college instead of accepting one of the three pro contracts that he received. A bunch of us wanted him to …" She straightened and abruptly interrupted what she was saying in mid-sentence as Mr. Bloomstack came back toward the service window. "Those kielbasa hot dogs are the best, don't you agree, Dan?" she said with a wink. "Are you planning on an ice cream bar for dessert, or maybe an orange cream rocket?"

Dan understood and played along. "I'll have a chocolate bar, please," he responded with a big smile.

"A chocolate bar it is then. What kind would you like?"

"The biggest one you've got."

Mr. Bloomstack was passing the boxes of chocolate bars and grabbed one from the rack and smacked it down in front of Dan. "There you go."

"How many of these do you sell a night, Mr. Bloomstack?"

"A dozen, if I'm lucky."

"What if I could double that amount for you?"

Mr. Bloomstack let out a deep belly laugh. "I'd say you would put on a lot of weight before the summer was over."

Dan's temper surged. His ears started to redden. He could feel his face begin to flush. Then, like a cooling breeze, he remembered: Separate the people from the problem, separate the people from the problem, …

Dan took a deep breath and tried to play it cool. "I'll tell you what, Mr. B, how about if I sell your peanuts and caramel corn at the same time I'm selling my team's chocolate bars?"

"I have no complaint if you want to sell my peanuts and caramel corn, but if they buy your chocolate bars, they won't be hungry enough to buy my peanuts and caramel corn."

"How many bags of peanuts and caramel corn do you sell in a game?" Dan asked.

Mrs. Bloomstack responded, "Maybe 20 bags of peanuts and a dozen bags of caramel corn."

"Is that pretty normal?"

Mr. Bloomstack scratched his ear. "You workin' for the Internal Revenue Service now, boy?"

"No, sir, but I'd like to work for you. I don't mean during the time we're trying to raise money for our team, but I could work the outlying diamonds for you for free, for a week after our contest is over."

Mr. Bloomstack shook his head in disbelief.

Dan continued, "Once people see how neat it is to buy stuff without walking all the way over here and missin' an inning of the game, you'll have a whole bunch of new customers. If I can't double your chocolate bar, peanut, and caramel corn sales the first week, I'll work free a second week."

"Can you believe this kid, Sally? This must be Daddy Bigbucks himself."

Dan saw Mr. Bloomstack's eyes twinkle. He sensed he would deal. Now was the time to sweeten his position. "One other thing, Mr. B, I'd sure find it mighty fair if you agreed to pay me a commission on all sales that go beyond that doubling point."

Mr. Bloomstack took a step back, as if a huge gust of wind had just hit him full force. He put his hands to his head and turned away. Dan's stomach knotted. He had had the deal; he knew he had the deal. What had come into his head? Why did he throw that commission thing in at the last minute and spoil everything?

Mr. Bloomstack turned back to face Dan.

"You win, kid, you win. You can sell your chocolate bars at the outlying diamonds until your fundraiser is over, but then you promise to work *free* for me for the next week selling *my* chocolate bars and *my* peanuts and *my* caramel corn."

"What about that commission issue?" Mrs. Bloomstack asked.

Mr. Bloomstack gave his wife a sideways glance and a raised eyebrow. Then he looked back at Dan. "What about it, Mr. Dan Martin? Does 10 percent strike you as fair?"

"Yes, sir!" Dan put his hand forward to shake on the deal, but Mr. Bloomstack didn't reciprocate. Instead, he placed both hands palm down on the counter. Dan instinctively straightened, but he didn't step back. Mr. Bloomstack squinted hard into Dan's eyes. "It's not a deal *yet*. I have some conditions of my own."

Dan was surprised, but he tried not to show it. "Yes, sir," he said in his most business-like manner. "I thought you might."

"You'll have to bring me your working papers, and you'll have to show me you know how to count change. I won't have a nitwit workin' for me that needs a cash register to calculate the correct change."

Dan wasn't sure what working papers were, but he figured Grant would know. About the change thing, he already understood that pretty well, and he'd practice over the weekend. Dan extended his hand a second time. "It's a deal."

Mr. Bloomstack gave Dan's hand a firm squeeze. With his left hand, he tousled Dan's hair. Then he turned toward the back room. Over his shoulder he called, "See you at 3 o'clock sharp on Tuesday, Daddy Bigbucks."

CHAPTER NINE
WHO, WHAT, WHERE …?

Grant came thundering up the steps two at a time and burst into Dan's room.

"What gives you the right to bust in here without knocking?" Dan challenged.

"Yeah, well, how'd it go with old man Bloomstack?"

"You want it play by play, or the final score?"

"Final score, then play-by-play."

"It was triple tough, but I'm in business starting Tuesday."

"All right!" Grant gave Dan a high five. "Sidewinder owes me a fiver. I knew I'd win that bet. So, how'ja manage it?"

Grant's eyes bugged as Dan gave him a play-by-play of his Bloomstack negotiations.

"Man, that was like hittin' a home run with the bases loaded. Considerin' what you've been through, you need to make sure there are no flub-ups."

"What's to flub up? I'm only selling three cartons of chocolate bars."

"Yeah, you can sell just the chocolate bars, or you can take this opportunity you've worked so hard for to the next level. It's your choice."

"What da'ya mean the next level?"

"Develop a project plan."

"What's that, and what's it gonna cost me?"

"Nothin'. I won't be around to coach you. I'll be in Omaha. I'll give you the general idea, but then you're on your own. Trial and error. A little like how you learned to play baseball before you had a coach."

"So what's a project plan?"

"It's a lotta stuff. Goals, strategies, tactics. You throw your goals out there, see, then you figure out the strategies you'll use to reach those goals, and then you use tactics to implement your strategies, and you keep drillin' down. Circles within circles." Grant was really getting into it. His words were almost falling over one another. "You're gonna love it."

Dan groaned. "You've lost me, man. I have no idea where you're comin' from. This is too much thinkin' for me."

Grant slowed down. "Loosen up, it's no different than baseball. Baseball's a thinkin' man's game, that's why you're good at it. It's the same with business. It's a thinkin' man's game, you'll be good at that, too. Business is the same as baseball. They're both about goals, strategies, tactics. To put it another way: Decisions, decisions, decisions."

"Not the baseball I play."

Grant looked annoyed. "Bull. As a pitcher you're thinkin' goals, strategies, tactics every minute you're on the field. It's just that you don't recognize it. You've been playin' baseball so long you shortcut to your decisions without even thinkin' about the goals, strategies, and tactics that got you to your decisions. Do you get on the pitcher's mound and just throw the ball any old way?"

"Of course not." Dan was incredulous.

"Why do you care how you throw the ball?"

"Cause I want to win."

"Okay, then one of your goals is to win. One of your strategies to reach that goal might be to strike out as many guys as you can. One of your tactics under that strategy might be to learn how to pitch an inside curve ball."

"A curve ball is a tactic?"

"Yeah, or it could be a goal or it could be a strategy."

"Which is it?"

"Yeah, well, it's kinda complicated. It took me months to figure it out, but you're a quick study. You'll probably get it quicker than me. You have lots of goals right?"

Dan nodded.

"Strategies are your plans for how you'll reach your goal."

"So why don't you just say plan instead of strategy? I know what it is to plan."

"Good question. Guess you could, but that's not playin' the game. Business types use the word 'strategies.' So when you play the business game, you need to use the word 'strategy'."

"Okay, got it. So what's a tactic?"

Grant smiled. "What do you think it might be?"

"I don't know. If strategies are used to reach your goals, maybe your tactics are used to reach your strategies."

"Right on, man! I like the way you reason. You're really cut out for this business stuff. Another way to say that is your tactics are your step-by-step actions. So back to the curve-ball thing. If your goal is to win the game, your strategy might be to strike the batter out, and your tactic might be to throw a curve ball. Agreed?"

Dan sat thinking.

"Say yes," Grant ordered.

"Yes," Dan complied.

Grant continued. He raised an eyebrow and his index finger. "But if you didn't know how to throw a curve ball, then you might make learning how to do that your goal. So if you have a new goal, then your strategies and tactics will change, right?"

Dan nodded.

"So if your new goal is to learn to throw a curve ball, what could one of your strategies be?"

Dan thought for a bit, "I could get a 'how-to' video from the library, or a book, or maybe I'd just ask Bob Carlsen how to throw a curve."

"Right, and what could one of your tactics be?"

"Tactics are actions, right?"

"Yeah."

"I might play the video again and again, practicin' until I got it down pat."

"You got it. Then you could even drill down, and refine that. You could set a new goal like improving your inside curve. Your strategy might be to study a video, and the tactic might be to kaizen your finger placement."

Dan nodded. "So goal, plan, action is really the same as goal, strategy, and tactics. Right?"

"Right! Talkin' business, is like talkin' baseball, or French, or Chinese, or any other language. When in Rome do as the Romans do."

Dan stretched his arms toward the ceiling and twisted his body. He got the picture and was ready to move on. "Is business as fast-paced as baseball? Am I gonna have to be constantly makin' decisions?"

"Wha'da'ya mean?"

"Well, in baseball I have to decide what type of pitch I'm gonna make, and that depends on things like if it's a close game, or if there's a runner on one of the bases. And then the split-second the ball leaves my hand, I'm no longer a pitcher, I'm an infielder, and Coach Tisdale says, before I pitch a ball I'd better know where I'll relay it, 'cause I might end up being the one that fields it."

Grant nodded. "That's the idea. The ball may never come your way, but if it does, you're prepared. That's what a project plan does. It prepares you to think about goals, and recognize the strategies and tactics you'll need in different situations. Good business strategy and good baseball strategy both require thinkin' ahead and plannin'."

"So a project plan is thinking ahead," Dan said confidently.

"In part, but there's a lot of lookin' backwards too. You know how you study the statistics of the other team before every game? You know a lot about each player's history before they get into the batter's box, right? Why do you do that?"

"So I won't pitch the kind of balls they find easy to hit. The more I know about a batter, the better my chances for success."

"The same with business. The more you know about your competition and your customers, the better your chances for success. Do you always pitch the same way?"

"Of course not."

"Why not?"

"Not every batter has the same skills. I'm not gonna exhaust my arm pitchin' a fast ball to a guy who can't hit, and if a guy can hit, I want to keep him guessin' about what might be comin' next. It also matters what the count is, if ..."

Grant interrupted. "So what you're tellin' me is you're constantly makin' decisions. Business is the same way."

Dan leaned back in his desk chair. "I guess I like decisions. So, what are some business decisions?"

"Your goal is to sell your chocolate bars. You have to have your customers connect with your sales pitch. You're pitching ideas. Get it?" Grant chuckled at his own pun and gave Dan a light tap to the side of the head with his open palm. "There are lots of sales pitches, and each one requires a different technique. The same pitch won't work on every customer. You need to be able to size up your customer the same as you size up your batters. Agreed?"

"Are you talkin' sellin emotion again?"

"Yeah, but you aren't pitchin' just raw emotion, you have to package it. Your delivery is important. Not just your advertising, but also how you treat your customer, and the quality of what you sell them. But I've gotten us off track. We started out talking project plans."

Dan smiled. He was starting to see how business could be a game. "So tell me more about project plans."

"Think of it as your game plan. You already have your goal—to sell three cartons of chocolate bars. You already decided on your strategy; you're gonna sell at the outlying diamonds at Stewart Park. So now you have to be sure you have considered all the aspects of your tactics."

"Those are my actions, right?"

"For every tactic you'll want to consider who, what, where, when, why, how, how many, how much, how long."

"What's the difference between how much and how many?"

"How much is money. How many is the number of things you have or need."

"Hold on," Dan complained. "This is getting too complicated again. How am I going to remember all that who, what, whatever stuff?"

"Memorize it."

"No thanks."

"Statistics say you're stupid if you don't. Without a project plan the odds aren't good."

"That's no skin off my nose. I'm not starting a business; I'm only sellin' chocolate bars for two more weeks."

"Man, when you went through all that stuff with old man Bloomstack, I thought you were motivated. This chocolate bar thing may be only a sandlot business, but it's the skills you begin learning in the sandlot that get you to the major leagues." Grant turned his back and walked out of the room.

"Wait up," Dan called. "You can tell me more about these project plans."

"Are you sure? I don't wanna be wastin' my time."

"I'm sure," Dan said with conviction.

Grant came back and sat on the edge of the bed. "Project plans are constantly changing to reflect real-world realities. Sometimes you plan for one thing, and it fails, and you have to make unplanned changes. Take your negotiations with Mr. Bloomstack, for example."

"Yeah, but I didn't have a project plan."

"That's true, but you could have had a project plan and still failed because of some small detail you didn't think about ahead of time. Project plans do not guarantee success; they only increase your probability of success.

Grant paused to let that sink in, then continued, "I consider my project plans as early warning systems. It gives me the opportunity to consider details in a systematic way.

By asking myself who, what, where, when, why, how, how many, how much, how long, I seldom have to cope with the unexpected, and when I do, my "who – what" system helps me reason out the best solution."

"You mean it's kinda like the pre-game check sheet you helped me make?"

"You could say that. A project plan is like a high-powered check sheet. It is all in the details. You try to think about everything. That doesn't mean it's always possible to fill in all the blanks, but with that list at least you're sure to consider it."

Dan's eyes sparkled with comprehension. "I got it." He swirled in his chair to face his computer. "Give me that list again. What came after who, and what?"

CHAPTER TEN
DON'T MOVE A MUSCLE

A lot had happened over the weekend. When Dan showed up for practice on Monday, everything appeared the same, and yet it felt different. He couldn't quite put his finger on what had changed.

Coach Tisdale called him aside. "How's the shoulder?"

"Feels fine, Coach. There's still a bruise, but no pain."

"Doc said no pitching for at least a week. He suggested I give you some isometrics."

"Does it taste bad?"

Coach laughed. "Isometrics are exercises to keep your muscles toned until you can get back into your regular routine. Carlsen's prepared to walk you through the process, and make sure you get the techniques down pat. Just take it nice and easy."

The two boys were developing a solid working relationship. Practice was a rewarding experience for both of them. Carlsen enjoyed coaching, and Dan loved learning how to become a more accomplished pitcher.

Carlsen put his arm around Dan's shoulder, "Okay Big D, here's the deal. Coach wants to keep your neck, shoulder, and arm muscles toned, but he can't risk having you put them through a full range of motion. The trick to isometrics is, don't move a muscle."

"You're pullin' my leg right? How can I exercise without moving a muscle?"

"You don't want to aggravate your injury. That will just keep you off the mound even longer."

"How can I possibly injure myself if I don't move a muscle?"

"Let me count the ways: by not framing your body properly, by applying maximum pressure too quickly, by holding a position too long, by doing too many repetitions…."

"Whoa man, you got my attention. So what's it mean to frame my body properly?"

"Make it picture perfect. Get it? Frame? Picture?"

Carlsen laughed at his own joke, and then continued, "Place your feet about hip-width apart, tuck your hips in, shoulders back, chin in, head tall. Perfect!"

"It's like being at attention."

"Whatever. Now put the palms of your hands together with your fingers pointing up. That's right. Now raise your elbows until they are even with your shoulders. Without moving, slowly press one hand firmly against the other. Are you feeling tension?"

"Yeah."

"Breathe normally; don't hold your breath. Good. Now relax, and put your arms down to your sides. That's it."

"That's it, that's all?"

"Right."

Dan was skeptical. "That seems way too easy to do much good."

"That's the beauty of isometrics. Slow and easy. Coach says if we do them right, we will get explosive speed when we hurl, and more power when we bat."

"I'm for that."

"So shut up and pay attention. We're gonna tense a muscle group six seconds, and then relax four seconds. We'll do four repetitions of each exercise."

Dan acknowledged, "6-4-4. Got it."

"Okay, repeat what you just did three more times. Press, two, three, four, five, six. Relax, two, three, four. Press …"

"I'm not breaking a sweat. I could do this all day."

"That would be a big mistake. Right now, more than four repetitions would be bad for your body."

"You're the coach."

"It's like I keep tellin' ya, practice is not about how many, it's about the right technique. With isometrics, always think equal and opposite. You just finished a push exercise. What's the opposite of push?"

"Pull?"

"You got it. Elbows up, clasp your fingers in front of you and pull. Nice and easy. Never long, and never many. Remember, 6-4-4."

Unlike most things, isometrics didn't require a lot of work for Dan to learn. By the time Coach Tisdale called the teams to the *Talking Tree*, Carlsen had led Dan through an entire series designed to tone his arms, shoulders, and neck muscles.

As they walked toward the *Talking Tree*, Dan said, "It seems neat that something so quick and easy can keep my muscles toned, and I don't even need special equipment."

"Want to know something else that's neat. Most people will never know you're doing isometrics, even if you're right in front of them. That's one secret-to-success that comes without the heat."

"What heat?"

Carlsen stopped and looked at Dan as if he were sizing him up. Finally he said, "Yeah, okay, if you have the balls, meet me at 7 tonight at the Hutchinson Dance Studio."

Then he turned and trotted up the hill toward the *Talking Tree*.

Dan let out a sharp breath. Was Carlsen kidding? He seemed serious. What could a ballet school for girls possibly have to do with power pitching? Carlsen never impressed Dan as a ballet kind of guy, but then again he didn't know him all that well. Dan wondered, what if someone saw him going in or out of the dance studio, how could he explain that? He batted the idea back and forth like a ping pong ball for the next hour, but still couldn't come to a decision about whether to meet Carlsen at 7 or not.

When Dan got home he went straight to Grant's room. He knocked the secret knock before he remembered Grant was in Omaha. He went to his room, sat down at his computer to chat with Grant, but got back an automatic message saying Grant was traveling and wouldn't be answering his email until tomorrow. Dan would just have to figure this out on his own.

He picked up his glove and baseball, and plopped on his back across his bed. He began to toss the baseball back and forth between his hands while his mind tried to solve his dilemma. He was still trying to put his finger on why things felt different today at practice. Then it came to him. Over the past week he had been on a big learning curve, and he was loving it. He wasn't the same person he was a week ago. His confidence had grown.

He rolled onto his stomach. Why was he second-guessing an opportunity to learn how to put more power into his pitches? When he thought about it, really thought about it, he knew deep down that he had enough confidence in himself to do this. He would definitely meet Carlsen tonight, no two ways about it.

As he approached the dance studio, his resolve started to weaken. He peddled by slowly, trying to get a glance of what was happening inside. The lights were on, but he couldn't see anyone. He rode around the block and looked in a second time. This time he got a glimpse of Madeline Hutchinson, the director of the studio, and the back of some guy's head. It wasn't Carlsen. That meant if he went in now, someone other than Carlsen would know about it. He went around the block again, and this time the room seemed empty. He parked his bike in the next block and walked back to the studio. He looked up and down the street, and not seeing anyone he knew, ducked inside.

The reception room was strewn with sneakers, jeans, and sweatshirts. The sound of a woman's voice came from the next room. "Stretch, two, three, four, five, and relax, that's twelve. And stretch, two, three, four, five, and relax, that's thirteen. And stretch, …"

Dan looked through the doorway. Miss Hutchinson saw him immediately, smiled, and without stopping her counting, motioned for him to come to her. He tried to size up the situation. Five guys he recognized from the varsity team were lined up doing stretches next to a bar. He was amazed to see them in tights, and wearing soft shoe slippers. Carlsen smiled, and cocked his head toward Miss Hutchinson. Dan moved hesitantly in her direction. When she finished the sixteen count, she held out her hand to Dan. "You must be Dan Martin."

"Yes, ma'am."

"Robert told me he had invited you to come this evening; we're glad you could make it. This group is too advanced for you to join, but you're welcome to watch and when class is over, we'll talk."

Dan took a seat on a bench along the wall opposite a large mirror. For nearly an hour, he watched the five work out. Their tights really pronounced their muscles. He could see their gluteus, hamstrings, and quadriceps at work. The similarities between ballet and pitching surprised him. There was stretch, balance, push, lift, and rhythm. Miss Hutchinson was a stickler for perfect form. She would correct how they held their heads, or how they pushed off into a jump, and how they landed, how their bodies twisted in a turn. She really worked the guys hard.

When they finished, Carlsen came over to where Dan was sitting. "Now you know our secret; what do you think?" He picked up a towel and wiped the sweat off his body.

"I think I see the connection."

"That's good; most guys don't. That's why we have a competitive edge." Carlsen sat down next to him on the bench.

As the other four guys passed them on the way to the reception room to claim their jeans and tennis shoes, they each offered Dan words of encouragement. When the others had left, Miss Hutchinson invited Dan and Carlsen into her office. There was nothing in it except a desk, three chairs, and dozens upon dozens of photographs. They were jammed so close, their frames touched, and in some cases overlapped. Miss Hutchinson closed the door for privacy. "Robert tells me you want to get more power behind your pitching."

"Yes, ma'am."

"I can help, but for me to be willing to do that, I have to know you have a strong commitment. Robert tells me you have talent, but that's never enough. The question is, do you have the fire in the belly?"

"I don't mind hard work."

"That's good. Robert can attest that ballet is physically demanding."

Carlsen let out a grunt. "That's an understatement. She'll work you 'til you drop."

Miss Hutchinson laughed. "You obviously love it. You keep coming back for more." She turned to Dan. "This is a tougher question. Do you think you have a mindset that can take the snide remarks some of your classmates might make when they hear you are taking ballet lessons?"

Dan squirmed in his seat. "I'll be honest. I didn't find it easy comin' here. I parked my bike a block away and kinda snuck in. But that was before I knew what ballet really was."

"What difference does knowing make?"

"I'm not sure; I can see a lot that's like pitchin'."

"Like pitching? How so?" she asked.

"You know, I mean, like stretching, and balance, and push, and rhythm, and stuff like that."

"You saw all that?" There was true admiration in her voice. "Usually, I have to explain that to athletes, and you saw it on your own. That's very encouraging." She turned to Carlsen. "You were right. He is mature for his age. I'll grant your request."

Then she turned back to Dan. "Here's the deal. I'll start you at two times a week for half an hour each. You have to pay for your lessons out of your own money. If you don't get an allowance, or don't have a job, I'll find you some work. But I'm insistent that you have to pay your own way. If I feel you aren't taking your lessons seriously, then it's over. Are you prepared to live with that?"

"Yes, ma'am! I have an allowance, I have some savings, and I may be earning some commissions."

"Commissions?"

"I've worked out a deal with Mr. Bloomstack at Stewart Park to sell chocolate bars."

"Well, if Ralph has decided to mentor you, I have no doubt you're worth my gamble. Will Mondays and Fridays at 6:30 work for you?

"Absolutely!"

"Good." She opened a desk drawer and took out a picture and handed it to Dan. "You may find this will get you through some difficult times. Robert can tell you about it." She stood as a signal that the meeting was over.

"Thank you, I'll be here on Monday at 6:30 sharp."

Dan walked with Carlsen into the waiting room.

"Congratulations. You're gonna reach a whole new level."

"Thanks for vouching for me. I won't let you down."

"I know you won't. That's why I asked her. Do you know what that picture is?"

"It looks like some ballet."

"It's the Nutcracker ballet. Those dancers are members of the San Diego Padres."

"For real?"

"For real! It was a fund-raiser for charity."

"Man, I can't believe this week. I'm the luckiest guy in the world."

Dan's life was on a roll. Things just seemed better day after day. He was back on the pitcher's mound. He sold his entire inventory of chocolate bars in just two days. And surprisingly, he discovered he really liked Mr. Bloomstack and was looking forward to working for him for a week or two, even if he didn't make any money.

Dan arrived at the concession stand early the next day. "This may surprise you Mr. B.; I've sold all my chocolate bars and am ready to honor our agreement," Dan said with considerable pride.

Mr. Bloomstack was impressed. "You're a good businessman. You're organized and you pay attention to detail. I like that."

"Thanks. Grant got me started on project planning before he left for Omaha. All that who, what, where stuff makes it pretty easy to be organized."

"Tisdale tells me Grant's a good man."

"Yeah, I really miss him. Talkin' by email isn't the same. When do you want me to begin Mr. B?"

Mr. Bloomstack began to wipe down his counter, then he turned to Dan. "I've been thinkin'; you negotiated with me to sell your team's chocolate bars for two weeks. Your time's not up, so if you like, you can ask Coach Tisdale for more inventory and finish out the two weeks."

"Really? That's great, Mr. B!" There was a long pause. Then Dan said, "My friends Chandler and Spider are having some trouble sellin' their chocolate bars."

"Are you suggesting I give them a chance to sell on the outer fields?"

"I guess you could say that."

"Talk about giving an inch. Now instead of just you giving me competition, you want an entire sales team."

"Hadn't thought of it that way."

"What's in it for me?"

Dan smiled. He could see Mr. Bloomstack was giving him a chance to negotiate. "What do you want?"

"I know what I don't want."

For a moment Dan was caught by surprise. Then the logic hit him. It was like the emotion thing Grant had taught him. Sometimes we buy things to feel good, and sometimes we buy things so we won't feel bad. It made sense that we could negotiate to get something we wanted, or to avoid something we didn't want.

"Okay, what don't you want?"

"I don't want a bunch of kids underfoot. I don't have time to train them or supervise them."

"How about if you never even see them. They work for me. I train them. I supervise them. They work only the outlying diamonds."

"I'll consider that. You write up something that states all the who, what's, and where's. It should say you'll be responsible for their training, their competence, and their conduct. If they're going to be selling chocolate bars at Stewart Park, I expect them to meet the standard you have already established. If we can agree in writing, then you're in business."

Dan was jubilant. "Yes, sir. I'll have a contract tomorrow."

"Not a contract. You're too young to legally sign a contract. We'll have a letter of understanding."

"Whatever you want to call it, you won't be sorry, Mr. B."

Chandler and Spider jumped at the chance to join Dan's sales team. Even Gabby, who had sold all of his chocolate bars, wanted to be part of the action. The rest of the two weeks went smoothly. Dan's sales team sold their assigned cartons of chocolate bars, and on three occasions asked Coach Tisdale for additional inventory.

When the contest was over Gabby, Spider, and Chandler offered to help Dan fulfill his obligation to Mr. Bloomstack, but Dan preferred to meet that challenge on his own. It wasn't hard; the crowds at the outlying diamonds had gotten used to the convenience of not having to walk to the concession stand for their snacks.

When Dan's last day of working for Mr. Bloomstack arrived, he knew he would miss seeing him everyday. As they were saying their good-byes, Mr. Bloomstack put his hand on Dan's shoulder. "You put in a pretty impressive performance the past two weeks, Mr. Dan Martin. How would you like to continue working for me the rest of the summer?"

"Really?" Dan asked excitedly. Then he caught himself, realizing he should negotiate. "What terms do you have in mind, sir?"

"I was thinkin' minimum wage to start with."

"Minimum wage is okay to start with. But how about adding a commission on sales?"

"I don't know. That could add up to quite a bit of money the way you have been goin'."

"Right, we'll both stand to gain."

"Alright, alright. I don't want to lose a good man over a small commission. Shall we say 5 percent?"

"I think we should keep it at 10 percent, the same as it has been."

Mr. Bloomstack stared up at the ceiling for nearly a minute. The silence made Dan nervous, but he remembered *Getting To Yes* said that if you have an offer on the table, be sure to keep silent and wait for a response. So Dan waited for what seemed forever. Finally, Mr. Bloomstack looked him in the eye. "Can I count on you to start next week?"

"Yes, sir."

"It's a deal. You draw up our agreement, and I'll sign it."

CHAPTER ELEVEN
PENNY PICKIN'

The next Saturday, Mr. Bloomstack handed Dan his first paycheck. "So, Daddy Bigbucks, just how are you planning to spend it?"

"Don't know, hadn't thought about it."

"Hadn't thought about it?" Mr. Bloomstack rolled his eyes. "Hadn't thought about it? You nag, nag, nag me to sell your chocolate bars; you build a sales team; you negotiate the terms for a regular job; you work your fanny off; and you don't even know what you'll do with your money?"

Dan shrugged.

"Alright, I'll bail you out. Sally, ya mind watchin' the stand for a few minutes? Mr. Dan Martin and I have some business to discuss." He put his arm around Dan's shoulder. "Let's go to the backroom for a man-to-man talk."

"I already had my man-to-man talk with Dad before he was sent to the Middle East, and Grant is always throwing in his two cents worth."

"Ya mean women?"

"Yeah."

"I learned a lo-o-o-ng time ago that I don't know enough about women to advise anyone, not even a young kid like you. We're gonna have a talk about money. That's somethin' I know a little somethin' about, and it seems to me your education is a bit wantin' in that area."

"Yes, sir," Dan said, figuring it was futile to resist. It was clear Mr. Bloomstack was going to have his say.

They sat down at the large round table that was a combination desk and conference table. Mr. Bloomstack tossed a yellow pad and pencil onto the leather rawhide that covered the table. "You might want to take notes; this is pretty important stuff. It's the difference between those who make it into the majors, and those who are stuck in the sandlot."

"Are we talking baseball or are we talking money?" Dan inquired.

"Yes!" Mr. Bloomstack responded. "We're talkin' game strategy. This is about the money game. If you're gonna be any good at it, it's the same as baseball; you hav'ta understand the playin' field, know the rules, and practice, practice, practice. Savvy?"

Dan looked at his check. "We aren't talkin' about a lot of money here, Mr. B."

"Money is money, boy, remember that. No matter how much you have, it can become a whole lot more if you play the game well. The bunt that gets you to first base can end up bringing you across home plate. The scoreboard will count it the same as if you had hit a home run. All money counts, no matter how much it is."

"Pennies don't count," Dan countered. "You can't buy anything with a penny anymore. I wouldn't even bend down to pick up a penny."

Mr. Bloomstack reached into his pocket, pulled out a penny, and flipped it to the floor. "You heard of compound interest, Mr. Know-It-All?"

Dan smiled sheepishly. "No, sir."

"Well, for a penny, I'll tell you about compound interest."

Dan could see the twinkle in Mr. Bloomstack's eyes. He wasted no time in bending over, picking up the penny, and slapping it on the table. "Here's your penny. What's the interesting thing you're going to tell me?"

"Compound interest," Mr. Bloomstack said emphatically.

"Okay. What's this compound interest?"

"Let's just suppose, for the sake of making my point, that this here penny is worth 2 cents tomorrow, and 4 cents the next day, and your money continues to double every day for a month. And let's say you could have all that money, *or* you could have my concession stand. Which would you take?"

"Wow, that's easy. I'd take your concession stand."

"You're sure of that, are you?"

"You mean this penny would be worth 2 cents tomorrow, 4 cents the next day, and 64 cents by the end of the week. Right?"

"Right, that's exactly what I mean. The first penny is your principal, and all the other pennies are your interest. You never spend any of it; you just keep reinvesting your initial principal and all your interest, and every day it doubles from the day before. Got it?"

"Yeah."

"You're sure you want my concession stand?"

"Right. I'd still take your concession stand."

Mr. Bloomstack rubbed his forehead with his fingers and studied Dan. Finally he asked, "What do you suppose this concession stand is worth?"

"Don't know, but it must be worth almost as much as some houses."

"That's true, the building is worth as much as some houses. But then, this isn't a house. It's a business. There's value in my equipment, and value in my inventory, and value in my good will. They're all worth money."

"Your good will?"

"My business' good name. Nowadays they call it 'brand equity.' There's value in all the customers that come to Ralph's because they know they can count on finding good stuff to eat, at a price they can afford, and are willing to pay."

"I guess you got plenty of brand equity, Mr. B.; your customers sure do keep me busy."

"We're agreed then; this concession stand has value in real estate, value in equipment, value in inventory, and value in brand equity. It's a pretty significant bundle, if I do say so myself. So for the third time, what will it be? This penny doubled for 30 days, or my concession stand?"

"For sure, your concession stand."

"That's three strikes and you're out! Here, take this calculator. Key in a penny. Now double it, and keep doubling your total 30 times and tell me what you get."

Mr. Bloomstack got up from the table and began to straighten shelves. After two minutes, Dan still hadn't given him an answer. Mr. Bloomstack peered over Dan's shoulder. "Well, wha'da'ya have?"

"I think you've given me a trick calculator."

"I've what?" Mr. Bloomstack laughed.

"This is a trick calculator, right?"

"Sally," yowled Mr. Bloomstack, "the kid thinks I've given him a trick calculator."

Mrs. Bloomstack peered around the corner. "What's all the fuss?"

"Dan here is trying to double a penny for 30 days, and he thinks I've given him a trick calculator."

"You're right to be suspicious of him, Dan. He's definitely a practical joker. Here," she reached up and took a calendar from the wall and handed it to Dan. "Better do it the old fashioned way using a paper and pencil."

Mr. Bloomstack complained. "You two make quite a team. How's a guy to win?"

He went back to his shelves, and Dan began to fill in the squares on the calendar. At the end of the second week, he wrote in $81.92. He chuckled to himself. He wasn't going to be snickered this time. At the end of week three, he began to squirm a little in his chair. That penny had doubled to over $10,000, and he still had nine days to go. When he reached day thirty, he leaned back and let out a huge sigh.

Mr. Bloomstack gave him a Cheshire cat smile. "Well, wha'da'ya have?"

"Over $5 million. I guess it wasn't a trick calculator after all," Dan admitted

"Neat, huh? It doesn't look like much at first, but then POW! So, you interested enough to want to learn more about the money game?"

"You better believe it!"

"Okay! This is a whole new inning. Here's a slow ball right down the middle. If you could have a penny, plus its interest, doubled every day for a month, or you could have my concession stand, which would you take?"

Dan laughed. "The penny plus its interest that is doubled every day for a month."

"That's more like it. By the way, if you ever find someone offering 100 percent a day compounding, let me know, I'm always lookin' for a miracle."

He sat down in his chair and leaned across the table with a serious look. "My example may not have been very realistic, Dan, but I'll bet dollars to donuts you'll remember there's value in a penny and what it means to compound your money."

"I'm not a gamblin' man, Mr. B., but just how many donuts is that to a dollar?"

Mr. Bloomstack rocked back on his chair and roared with laughter. He grabbed the table just before his chair tipped over backwards. "You got a head on your shoulders, boy. Here, take this penny and get it imbedded in one of those plastic key rings. It'll be kinda symbolic. Compound interest is one of the keys to your success in the money game."

"Thanks, Mr. B."

"Here's a more realistic problem for you to chomp on. Let's just say, for example, you save 20 percent of your paycheck, and you invest it so that the return on your investment is 6 percent a year compounded annually. You reinvest principal and interest until you're ready for college. What will it be worth then? Or let's say you don't use it for college, but decide to keep reinvesting it until you're 65. What will it be worth then?"

"Twenty percent of my paycheck. I can treat my friends to a movie and take in Jimmy's after, for that."

"Take it easy, you still have another 80 percent we can talk about tomorrow. You were the one who said you didn't know what you were going to do with your money. Let's keep focused here. Your project plan helped you to do a better job at making money. Tomorrow, we'll talk about your personal budget. A budget will help you to do a better job of spending the money you've earned. Savvy?"

Mr. Bloomstack opened his laptop. "Get along with you, it's time for me to mind my business."

Dan headed for the door. "I can't wait to email Grant about the penny trick."

"My guess is Grant already knows about compounding his money, but give it a try."

As the concession stand door slammed behind Dan, he positioned the penny on his left thumbnail and gave it a flip. The penny tumbled in a high arc. Dan caught it and slapped it onto the back of his right hand. He lifted his left hand a smidgen and snuck a peek. He threw his head back, squared his shoulders, and began walking with a bit of a swagger. A mantra repeated in his mind with every step. Heads up! Heads up! Heads up!

CHAPTER TWELVE
STICKS AND STONES

"Hey, man, glad I found you. Your cell's off. We've been callin' you for the last hour."

"It's always off when I'm at my dance class."

Gabby squeezed into the booth next to Dan. "Hey, don't say that so loud; someone will hear. I know why you're doin' it, but I don't want anyone to know I hang out with a guy who goes to ballet class."

"Gabby, sometimes you're so narrow-minded. Get over it."

"It's just weird."

"Come with me next time. You might just be surprised."

"Can it." Gabby looked around to see if anyone nearby could hear their conversation. "Listen, we were tryin' to reach you because Spider's old man is puttin' together a pickup game. He invited us guys to join him."

"No kiddin'? Where? When?"

"Right now, in the sandlot. They sent me over here to see who I could find. We couldn't reach you, and we're one man short."

"Why didn't you say so, let's go."

When Dan saw who was at the sandlot, he stopped short. "You sure we're invited? Geez, look, Coach Tisdale is even here."

Chandler came running. "Man, I thought you were gonna miss out on this. We've been tryin' to reach you forever."

Spider called from the field. "You guys better warm up, we'll be startin' soon. Hey, Gabby, heads up."

Gabby snatched the ball and tossed it to Dan. "Let's warm up."

Just after the bell on City Hall chimed the half hour, the umpire called, "Team draw."

Everyone ran toward home plate. As Dan approached to draw a slip of paper from the hat, he recognized the umpire. "Chandler, that's Bloomstack! I'm cuttin' out."

"Hey, it's not like you're crashin' the party. You were invited," Chandler reassured him.

Gabby sidled up next to Dan. "This is neat, really neat. We've been practicin' against the varsity team, and now we get to play with some of the guy's in the Men's League. Is this neat, or is this neat?"

"I'll tell you when the game's over." Dan turned to Spider. "I don't think I can pitch nine innings against these guys."

"You won't have to. You only pitch one out, then you rotate," Spider said,

"What's that mean?"

"Everybody plays every position. We rotate positions after every out. It goes from pitcher, to catcher, to first base, then second, shortstop, third, left field, center field, right field and back to pitcher."

"Got it. Sounds like fun." Dan turned to Gabby. "Yeah, you're right, this is pretty neat."

Mr. Bloomstack held the hat with the paper slips out to Dan. "Well, if it isn't Mr. Dan Martin. You didn't tell me you horsed around with the Men's League."

"I don't, I mean this is my first time." Dan drew the home team, and trotted toward the pitcher's mound where they were gathering.

Coach Tisdale held out his hand. "You're in the majors now, how does it feel?" He didn't wait for an answer. "I'm your teammate tonight, not your coach, so relax and have fun."

Dan smiled and nodded, but he felt conflicted inside. It was exciting to be playing with members of the Men's League, but it was also a lot of pressure having his coach for a teammate and his new boss as the umpire. His mind raced in search of reassurance. He grabbed on to the image of Bob Carlsen pitching his shutout. He transferred that image to himself: calm, cool, and competent. He took a deep breath, did 5 standing cobras to relax his shoulder muscles, and felt much better.

A guy that looked more like a line backer than a baseball player introduced himself. "I'm Chad Hansen; I'm the team captain for tonight. How would you like to pitch the first out of the game? Tisdale will be your catcher, and you'll rotate behind him."

"Yes, sir." Dan moved to the top of the mound, and Coach Tisdale headed toward home plate. The other players took the positions as Chad assigned them. Dan pitched four or five warm-ups.

"You're on tonight, Dan, nice, very nice," Coach Tisdale chattered.

"Batter up," Bloomstack called.

Dan pitched low inside. It was a little too inside. The batter stepped back. "Ball one." Dan's next hurl was over the plate for a strike. The batter missed the third pitch, but on the fourth he connected, and sent a fly to right field, where it was expertly snatched for the first out of the game.

Dan moved to the catcher's position, and then to first base. By the end of the first inning he was really into it. He was feeling very comfortable playing with the men. His turn to bat came at the beginning of the second inning. He hit a line drive that got past the second basemen, and was retrieved by the right fielder, but he managed to reach first base just before the ball. He worked his way around to third base before the third out.

Chandler, Dan, Spider, and Gabby were all playing well. Practice against the varsity team had prepared them for playing a pickup game with players from the Men's League.

Dan was in right field and Coach Tisdale was pitching at the top of the fourth. Coach had a one-one count when a guy they called Lucky hit a comebacker that nearly knocked Coach off his feet. He caught it, but he didn't relay it to first. Instead he started running toward first base, with both hands on his glove. Dan couldn't figure out what was happening. "Throw the ball. Throw the ball," he demanded, forgetting he was screaming orders at his coach. Tisdale suddenly threw his glove to the first baseman, who caught it just before the runner reached first base. Bloomstack didn't make a call. Instead, he grabbed the glove from the first baseman, examined it, and yelled, "You're out!" Then he doubled over in laughter.

The ball had come off Lucky's bat with such velocity that it had wedged into the webbing of Coach's glove, and he couldn't get it loose. So he started running toward first base, but when he saw Lucky was going to beat him there, he took off his glove and threw it to the first baseman. Lucky good-humoredly challenged the decision.

Bloomstack held firm on his verdict. He said his call had precedence, and cited the call made in the major leagues by umpire Ed Montague when Keith Hernandez slammed the ball back to Terry Mulholland.

Ralph Bloomstack stopped the game to give everyone a chance to examine Coach Tisdale's glove. That was the end of a normal ball game. After that there was a lot of razzing and kidding around. Nearly every inning had some sort of high jinks. It was almost as crazy as donkey ball.

In one inning, the first baseman stuck a ribbon into the back of a runner's pants. When the guy led off to steal second, it unfurled behind him. When he saw he wouldn't make second, he doubled back to first and tripped over the ribbon. The first baseman tagged him for an out.

Then another guy was caught trying to steal home. They ran him back and forth between third and home about five times, then someone threw a second ball to the third baseman, so the runner was dodging two balls. You couldn't keep track which one was the game ball, and which one was the phony. The guy finally just stopped and rolled over like a dead dog with his arms and legs in the air, and his chest heaving in laughter.

In another inning, a powerful batter hit the ball out of the park. As he began his leisurely trot around the bases, the catcher dug up home plate, and ran with it to right field. When the runner saw what was happening he started chasing home plate. They zigzagged all over the outfield. The catcher was getting winded, so he passed home plate to Chandler. With his youth and long legs it was no contest. Then the batter's teammates emptied out of the dugout and surrounded Chandler, who then threw home plate to Spider. The dugout guys swirled like a swam of bees and headed in Spider's direction. He managed to pass back to Chandler before both of them were tackled. The batter could finally tag home plate, and Bloomstack signaled safe. That gave a whole new meaning to the concept of stealing bases.

The funniest high jinks occurred when Spider's dad was on the mound. Chad Hansen came to the batter's box swinging a tree branch that still had some leaves on it. He was yelling he didn't have time to carve a bat. Spider's dad held up his index finger for a time-out, and walked off the field. He picked up a stone and held it up between his thumb and his forefinger for everyone to see. He wrapped his handkerchief around the stone, and then walked over and picked up the ribbon from the earlier inning. With great ceremony he wrapped the ribbon around and around the handkerchief before tying it off with an expert clove hitch. Both sides cheered as he walked back to the mound.

Bloomstack called, "Play ball."

Spider's dad pitched his stone ball, Chad Hansen swung his tree branch, and the ball lodged itself in a "Y" branch. Everyone roared. Chad threw the branch onto the diamond, and ran toward first. The catcher quickly grabbed the branch and ran after him. He managed to give Chad a swat on the butt before he reached the bag. That was the first out of that inning, but Bloomstack yelled, "That's game. Who's buying?"

Some said it should be Lucky, others insisted it had to be Chad, still others thought Spider's dad had earned the honor. Bloomstack settled it. "Everyone buys their own tonight, and I'll pay for the freshmen. They had no idea what they were getting into when they agreed to play with you guys."

There was a lot of camaraderie between the generations at Jimmy's that night, as the stories of the high jinks were told and retold as each new customer arrived.

CHAPTER THIRTEEN
THE GOLDEN EGG

The euphoria of success permeated every cell of Dan's body. Practice, ballet, work, everything was exceeding Dan's expectations. His confidence was growing every day.

"Morning, Mr. B. That was a wild game last night."

"You never know what to expect from those guys. They're crazy."

"Yeah, it was a lot of fun. I emailed Grant about it. He responded with a bunch of smiley faces. I told him you were gonna help me with budgeting today. He said I should take good notes, cause it's complicated and he's havin' some trouble with his budget right now."

"Take all the notes you like, but there will be some big differences between your budget and Grant's."

"You can say that again. Grant makes more than 10 times what I do."

"Budgeting isn't about the amount of money. It's about how you use the money you have. Grant is in a totally different place in his life than you are. He doesn't have the freedom of how to spend his money that you have."

"How so? The way I see it, his big check gives him a bunch more options."

"His income may be more, but so are his expenses now that he is living on his own in Omaha."

"Yeah, he was complainin' last night about the cost of his rent, food, and car. He said his taxes were almost 33% off-the-top, whatever that means."

"It means that his employer has withheld his state, federal taxes, and Social Security taxes from his paycheck.

Grant doesn't have any children or anyone else that he is responsible to care for, so his taxes are gonna be pretty high. The amount I withheld from your earnings is shown on your check stub."

Dan hadn't paid any attention to his check stub. He reached into his back pack, pulled it out and examined it. "Wow! Withholdings is a lot."

"Yup! And it's wise to take your savings off-the-top also," Mr. Bloomstack advised.

"I'm not sure about savings. Last night down at Jimmy's, Sidewinder was sayin' that savin' was for old married men. You should live it up while you're young."

"Why am I not surprised? Sidewinder never did understand the money game. My guess is, by the time he's a married man, he'll have so much debt that his only discretionary money will be the amount that appears after the decimal point on his paycheck."

Dan chuckled. "I don't know, Mr. B., Sidewinder doesn't seem to have any shortage of money. He's a big spender. The girls seem to like that."

"I guess there will always be people who think they can buy friends." Mr. Bloomstack tapped his finger on the table. Dan sensed he might be thinking about when Sidewinder had worked for him. It seemed to Dan that the time Mr. Bloomstack had invested in Sidewinder had been a poor investment.

Mr. Bloomstack looked up. "Let's get back to your budget. Make two columns. At the top of one write 'fixed costs'; at the top of the other write 'discretionary costs'. Your #1 item under your fixed costs is your retirement fund."

"Retirement? I'm only 14."

"Do you remember our discussions about compounding?"

"Okay, I get it. So how much do I put into retirement?"

"That's a good question. You just have to make a calculated guess. The experts say 20 percent of your pay check."

"Is that what you do?"

"My Dad started me at 20 percent when I was about your age. That seems to be working pretty well for me."

"You mean you've been putting 20 percent of your paycheck into your retirement account since you were 14?"

"I've mostly worked for myself, so I don't have a paycheck, but I did feed my retirement account 20% of my net income until my nest egg was large enough to ensure I wouldn't have a big change in lifestyle when I retired."

"What's good enough for you, Mr. B., is good enough for me. Make it 20 percent."

"Remember what we said when we started. Your personal budget is unique. It will be different from Grant's, and it will also be different from mine. The key point is good budgets are both simple and flexible."

"Flexible? You mean it's gonna change?"

"Well, the basic rules don't change. You always set a goal, and assign the goal a specific dollar amount, and set a time-frame to meet the goal. However, goals, dollars, and time can change. You have to be prepared to make adjustments."

"That has a familiar ring to it. Sounds a lot like project planning, right?"

"Any time you have planning, you have the opportunity for a game. You can make a game of baseball, business, or money." Mr. Bloomstack leaned back in his chair and cupped his head in his hands. "And somethin' else, no matter what game you're playin', you also have to be prepared to lose every now and then. You want to win. You expect to win. But ..."

Dan got the picture. "It's like baseball right? When you lose, you analyze what went wrong and figure out how to do better next time."

"You're good at lookin' around the corner, Dan. You have a sense of what's comin'."

"Thanks, but project planning, and budget planning are a whole lot harder than baseball."

"You think baseball was easy to learn?"

"Sure, everyone knows baseball."

"Everyone should know budgeting, too. I have to disagree with you about baseball being easy to learn. I think you've forgotten how hard it was. Watch a 2-year-old and see how many times they drop a ball tossed to them. Or watch a 5-year-old try to connect their bat with the ball, or how about a 9-year-old trying to decide what to do with the ball they just fielded. It has taken you years to develop into the player you are today, and I'm sure you'll agree you made a lot of mistakes along the way."

"Yeah, and still do."

Mr. Bloomstack laughed. "A mistake means you've been given an opportunity to learn. Take it from me, if you want to live an interesting life, you'll never turn out the light at night unless you've learned somethin' new that day."

"You mean I should make a mistake everyday?"

"That's not what I meant, and you know it."

Dan laughed. "Okay, what's next after retirement?"

"You tell me. What's important to you? What are your money goals?"

"I don't know. I don't have any."

"Hmmm. Then I guess our conversation about personal budgeting is over. Without goals, you might just as well dig a hole and pull your debt in on top of you."

"I'd like to go to a baseball camp next summer."

"Baseball camp, that's a good short term goal. You …"

Dan interrupted. "What do you mean short term? It's more than a year away."

"Time is relative. Let's call any savings that you intend to use in less than three years short term. How many months until you'll need to pay for baseball camp, and how much will you need?"

"It will cost about $200, and I'll need it in 14 months." Dan did the math. "I'll have to save $14.29 a month."

"Budgeting should be simple. For now, let's say your take-home pay is $100. That's a nice round number to use to calculate percentages. So baseball camp will be about 15 percent of your take-home pay. Do you put that in the fixed cost column or the discretionary column?"

"You said savings came off the top, so I guess it's the fixed cost column."

"Sorry, I wasn't clear. There are savings to build your nest egg, and there are savings to buy something that is expensive. Your nest egg should be a fixed cost. Fixed costs are necessities that are paid month after month. You have no choice. Things like your retirement nest egg, rent, heat, electricity, food, certain clothes, loans, and health insurance. Things that must be paid."

"I don't need to budget for those things. Mom pays for all that stuff."

"You get what I'm driving at. Is baseball camp really a necessity?"

"Not really." Dan moved the 15 percent for baseball camp to the discretionary column.

"When you're young you don't have many fixed costs, that's where Sidewinder is coming from. However, if you're smart, you'll start training for when you do, so let's put your college fund in the fixed cost column. Say 20 percent?"

Dan protested. "Mom's gonna pay for my college, and I'm hopin' I'll get a baseball scholarship."

"Those are both good things. If it turns out you don't need to use your college fund for college, you can always transfer those dollars toward another goal after you graduate. Agreed?"

"Agreed." The tone of Dan's voice made it clear it was a reluctant agreement. Dan looked at his sheet of paper: 20 percent for retirement, 15 percent for baseball camp, 20 percent for college. "We've only done three things and over half of my paycheck is gone already."

"It's not gone. It's just budgeted. Would you like to consider discretionary costs, things like contributions, investments, vacations, special projects, money to start a business, and of course, fun money?"

"Fun money sounds good."

"Whatever you say." Mr. Bloomstack said it in such a way that Dan knew he should be considering something else.

"What would you do?" Dan felt obliged to ask the question even though it was the fun money that really interested him.

Mr. Bloomstack eyeballed Dan. "You can work for money, or you can make money work for you. It's your choice. I'd budget for something that would put my money to work, to make me more money."

"Are you suggesting I should invest in my own business?"

"That's a good idea. I'll be closing the concession stand the first of October, so if you're going to meet your baseball camp goal by next summer, you're gonna have to find some other way to earn at least $15 a month until spring. I had my first business when I was your age. You're entrepreneurial. My guess is that sooner, rather than later, you're gonna want to give it a try, so it would be a good thing to start now to accumulate funds to cover as much of your start-up costs as you can. That will mean you'll have to borrow less when that time comes."

"Another 20 percent right?"

"Why don't we say 25 percent?"

"That leaves only 20 percent for fun money."

"Then let's put 10 percent for contributions, and that will leave 10 percent for fun money."

"You gotta be kidding, only 10 percent for fun money?"

"That's what I'm suggestin'."

"That stinks. From a $100 check, I only get to spend $10?"

"Eventually you'll spend the entire $100, plus the interest your savings will earn. You're just not going to spend it all next week. For instance, next summer you'll go to baseball camp with some of the money you earned last week. But until you're ready to use the money, you need to send it out to work for you. You don't want it sleepin' under your mattress doin' nothin'."

"I still think that stinks. I'll give it a try, but I'm pretty sure I'm gonna be makin' some adjustments next week."

"One more thing. I'm going to ask you not spend any of yesterday's paycheck until after you receive your next paycheck."

Dan was really annoyed now. "Jeez, I can't do that. I've already invited Chandler, Gabby, and Spider to the movies tonight to celebrate our success as a sales team. I can't back out now."

"You're right. I should have said something yesterday. This calls for an adjustment. Go ahead and celebrate with your sales team, but then don't spend another dime of this paycheck until you see your next paycheck. Savvy?"

"How come?"

"Because a portion of your income comes from commissions. Every paycheck is likely to be different. Sometimes your take home pay will go up, sometimes it will go down. If it goes up, no problem. However, if it goes down you'll have to make adjustments. It's gonna be much easier to make adjustments if you can average two paychecks rather than have it all come out of just one. It's always a good idea to keep a paycheck in reserve if you receive commissions."

"I still don't get it."

Mr. Bloomstack took some change out of his pocket and put it in two stacks. In one stack he put three dimes and two nickels. In the second stack he put two dimes and two nickels. "Pretend the three dimes and two nickels are this weeks earnings, but you don't spend it. Next week you earn the second pile. Are they equal?"

"No, the first one has 40 cents and the second one has only 30 cents."

"Right. You adjust them so they're equal. Then you disperse one pile according to your budget categories, and hold the other pile in reserve so you can adjust the following paycheck."

"I've got a better idea. I'm not gonna retire for a long time. If my income goes down next week, I just won't put any money in my retirement account."

"Well, Dan my boy, that is exactly what a lot of people do, but that's perhaps the worst decision you could make. There's that little thing called compound interest, remember?"

"I can always pay it back later."

"That's what people always tell themselves. Trust me, that's a slippery slope. It's better to train yourself from the get-go to never, never ever, borrow from your retirement fund."

"What about that flexible thing you talked about earlier?"

"Fixed costs aren't flexible. You can make your income flexible and your discretionary costs can be flexible, but fixed costs are just that. Fixed."

Dan studied his discretionary spending column. Mr. Bloomstack continued. "Look at it this way. This is your first paycheck. You've lived 15 years without one. You can manage one more week. Consider it insurance against cash-flow problems."

That got Dan's attention. "Cash-flow problems, that's what Grant said he had. He said he has a CD maturing next month, but for the next three weeks he has a cash-flow problem. I didn't know what he was talking about. I have a lot of CD's. They have nothin' to do with money, they just play music."

115

"Your CD's are compact discs. Grant's CD's are certificates of deposit. He loans money to the bank for a specific amount of time. In exchange for the money, the bank agrees to pay him interest. They give him a piece of paper, called a certificate of deposit. That CD allows him to reclaim all of his money, plus interest, on a certain date. But if he doesn't live up to his agreement and asks for his money back before the date, there's a penalty."

"Yeah, Grant explained that to me. He's having a rough time."

"Well, we'll try to see that you won't face that kind of a problem. Let's build a cash reserve into your budget as a safety cushion."

"There's no room in my budget for a cash reserve."

"Then we'll have to make some adjustments."

"Just from the discretionary column, right?"

Mr. Bloomstack nodded. Dan studied his spreadsheet. "We've got another problem here. You mentioned investments and I don't have an investment column either."

"You could consider your business start-up costs as an investment. You're investing in yourself."

"Does that mean baseball camp is also an investment?"

"If you like."

"That's a 40 percent investment in me."

"Actually, if you look at your spreadsheet closely, you're making a 90 percent investment in you. The only thing that is not for you is that little 10 percent contribution."

"I was considering changing that to be my cash reserve, but when you say it that way, I'd be pretty selfish if I didn't make contributions."

"I like your thinking."

"I'm not sure where to get money for a cash reserve. That must be Grant's problem, too."

"A cash reserve will certainly help Grant in the future, but right now, he will need a loan."

"He said he was gonna ask Mom for a loan, but he sure didn't want to."

"It's always good to have a 'banker' in the family, but Grant's right. It's better to never need a banker."

"Mom's not a banker, she's a dentist."

"Right, your mom's my dentist, but when she loans money to Grant, she's acting as Grant's banker." Mr. Bloomstack added, "One of my goals is to be my own banker. You might want to consider that to be one of your goals also."

"Grant gave me a baseball bank last year. I've been savin' some from my allowance, and some odd jobs. Grant told me I should buy a CD with that money, but now I'm glad I didn't; his CD hasn't helped him."

"Grant gave you good advice."

"If it was such good advice, why does he have to get a loan from Mom?"

"Grant doesn't have to get a loan from your mom; he could cash in his CD today if he had to. However, if he did, he would lose the interest he's been collecting. If instead, he borrows from your mom, and waits for his CD to mature, he can keep his CD money working for him. In the long run he will make money, but in the short run he has a cash-flow problem. Buying the CD wasn't Grant's mistake. His mistake was not creating a cash reserve."

"So there's nothing he can do now?"

"You can suggest he find himself a financial coach. Everybody can use a coach."

Dan was surprised. "Everybody? What about you, Mr. B.?"

"You better believe I have a financial coach. You ever watch the majors? How many coaches do you see on the field? There's not any game that I know of that a coach can't help a player improve."

"No question Mr. B., you're sure helpin' me." Dan shifted in his seat. "How about just using the money I already have in my baseball bank as my cash reserve?"

"You said you had enough to buy a CD, so that seems feasible."

"That's a relief. I sure didn't want to take it out of my fun money."

"Think about this one. Anytime your income is less than your expenses, you have two ways to balance your budget. You can reduce your expenses, or you can increase your income."

"Or you could do both, right?"

"Well, Daddy Bigbucks, no question about it. I like the way you use your mind to reason things out." Mr. Bloomstack pushed his chair away from the table indicating today's session was over. He squeezed Dan's shoulder as he got up. "When you decide you're gonna start a business, be sure to show me your business plan. I'd like to have the opportunity to be one of your investors, should you need one."

"Thanks, Coach." Dan's chest puffed. Grant was sure going to be surprised to hear this latest news. Dan was feeling so good that he temporarily forgot about having only 10 percent of his paycheck for fun money.

CHAPTER FOURTEEN
THE CATCHER

Dan sat on home bench, bouncing his legs up and down like a jackhammer. He swirled 360 degrees. Sidewinder was nowhere in sight. This was the second time he had agreed to catch for Dan and hadn't shown up. It was a straight-out insult, no two ways about it. Sidewinder just couldn't be relied on. Dan got up, walked to the outfield, and went through his warm-up exercises. He then ran the bases until he was out of breath, and then stretched out full length on the grass near the third base line. He closed his eyes and began to review the signals that Bob Carlsen had been teaching him.

He hadn't finished when Mr. Bloomstack's voice broke his concentration. "What'cha doin' out here, boy, pushing up daisies?"

Dan sprang to his feet. "Hi Mr. B. Want to catch a few?"

"Do I look like a catcher?"

"No, sir, you look like a pitcher."

"I do, do I? Well that's a fine how'da'ya do. We got two pitchers and no catchers."

"I'll catch for you Mr. B." Dan ran to home plate.

"Are you plannin' to catch at the state tournament?"

"No, sir, I'm plannin' on pitchin'."

"So why aren't you practicin' pitchin'?"

"Sidewinder didn't make it."

"Sidewinder has always had a problem with reliability." Dan shrugged.

Mr. Bloomstack continued, "Seems to me if you're plannin' to pitch at the state tournament, you need a more reliable friend."

"Yeah. Well, he isn't really a friend. He's older than I am."

"Maybe older in years, but he's certainly not as mature. It's clear that in terms of reliability he's a lot younger. I'll tell you what. You be here at 6:30 tomorrow morning, and I'll introduce you to the friend I pitched to 40 years ago."

"Your friend still works with pitchers?"

"Let's just say my friend has aged better than I have."

"I didn't mean ..."

"No offense, I know what you meant. I also know you need a friend you can count on, one that will be there any-time you decide you want to practice. Not an on-again, off-again unreliable sort."

"For real, Mr. B., you have a friend that will practice with me?"

Mr. Bloomstack chuckled. "You got wax in your ears, boy?"

"FANTASTIC!" Dan gave Mr. Bloomstack a high five. "Race you to concession stand."

"I'm too tired for that. You race; I'll watch."

The next morning Dan's alarm clock rang at 5:30. He awoke encased like a cocoon inside of his bed sheets. Squirming, he managed to free an arm and silence the clock with a firm wallop from his open palm. Dan contin-ued rocking from side to side, and up and down, until he managed to break free from his sheet. Breathing hard, he spread-eagled himself across his now coverless bed and closed his eyes. When he opened them again it was 6:20.

Dan didn't take time to wash the sleep from his eyes, brush his teeth, or eat breakfast. Even so, he was a couple of minutes late getting to the park. To his relief, Mr. Bloomstack was alone outside the concession stand. His friend was nowhere in sight. Dan skidded his bike to a stop and leaned it against the wall. "Sorry to be late, I'm sure glad your friend's late too."

"Well, you got it half right. You're late."

"Yeah, I overslept."

"I don't want to hear any excuses. It doesn't make any difference *why* you're late. Late is late."

Dan nodded. He remembered Grant's story about Mr. Bloomstack and the bus. The friend, like the bus, must have left when Dan hadn't arrived on time. He dropped to the ground.

Mr. Bloomstack's eyes twinkled. "The good thing is, you've got all day to figure out how to make sure it won't happen again. Savvy?"

"Yes, sir."

"Good, but like I said, you got it only half right. My friend was here before I was. You're just lucky my friend's not the kind to take offense because you're a lug-a-bed."

Dan smiled sheepishly.

"Come on," Mr. Bloomstack commanded and walked up to the sidewall of the concession stand. "Wall, I'd like you to meet Mr. Dan Martin. He'd like you to help him become a crackerjack of a pitcher. Dan, meet my good friend, Wall."

"Your friend's a wall?" Dan asked incredulously.

"That's right, and Wall here is about to become your best friend, too."

"I don't get it. I thought you said you were going to get someone for me to pitch to."

"I didn't say someone, I said a friend. Well, Wall here, is your friend. Watch this."

Mr. Bloomstack stepped back a few feet from the wall and pitched a slow ball. It hit the wall and rebounded back to him. He pitched another and another. Then he smiled his 'gotcha' smile and handed the ball to Dan. "You try it."

Dan knew he'd been had. He took the ball and gave it a toss and got the same result. "This is neat! You have a real awesome friend, Mr. B."

"You haven't seen the half of it. Wall here is a perfect umpire. Never makes a wrong call."

"How's that?" Dan had no doubt he was about to have another surprise.

"Well, where do you have to pitch a ball to have the umpire call a strike?"

"Over home plate, no higher than the batter's arm pits and no lower than his knees."

"Right. Are you pretty average height for your league?"

"I guess, maybe a little taller."

"Come position yourself like a batter."

Dan did as he was told and sidled up to the wall. Mr. Bloomstack took a roll of duct tape from his pocket, tore off a strip, and fastened it to the wall at the point just below Dan's knees. He tore a second strip off the roll and fastened it to the wall at the level of Dan's armpits. Then he handed Dan the tape. "Okay, I've done half, you do the other half."

Dan wasn't positive what the other half was, but he had a pretty good inkling, and knew Mr. Bloomstack expected him to know. He looked at the wall, then at Mr. Bloomstack, and then back at the wall. He turned to ask a question and saw the screen door to the concession stand close behind Mr. Bloomstack.

Realizing he was on his own, Dan began to formulate his own plan. It seemed pretty obvious to him that he was supposed to create a strike zone, so he placed the end of the roll of duct tape at the armpit line and unrolled it until it reached the knee tape. Then he took out his pocketknife, and cut the duct tape at exactly that point, and then repeated the same process a few inches to the right. When he finished, the strike zone looked too narrow.

Not having a tape measure, Dan ran over to Diamond 2, unrolled the tape across home plate, and cut it to the exact length. With this perfect measure, he ran back to the wall and readjusted the second vertical stripe. After carefully trimming all the edges, he stood back to admire his work.

"Purr..fection!" "Purr..fection!" "Purr..fection!" he chanted as he strutted to pick up the ball and resume practice. Wall was the perfect umpire. Three balls, one strike. Not exactly what Dan was hoping for. "Hey Wall, this one's going to be a strike," Dan called, but it contacted the wall high outside. "That was close. Let's call it a strike." Dan knew he couldn't really fool himself. "Okay, Wall, have it your way, ball four, the batter walks."

Dan had a good workout with Wall. One thing was very different, however. Wall wasn't open to influence the way Gabby always was. He could plead and bargain with Gabby, and close ones were always called in Dan's favor. But, he wasn't able to bias Wall. Under no circumstance would Wall cut him any slack. In that respect, Wall, Coach Tisdale, and Mr. Bloomstack were very much alike.

The concession screen door slapped closed and Dan turned to see Mr. Bloomstack coming toward him with a couple of large cups. "Need a lemonade break?"

"Sounds good."

"Just what do you think of your new friend?"

"Not what I expected, Mr. B, but I gotta admit your friend's real neat."

They walked over to a shady spot and sat down. "Did you forget your jacket?"

"Naw, it was already in the high 70s by the time I left home. Figured I wouldn't need a jacket today."

"Mine's hangin' next to the freezer door. It may be a little big for you, but you're welcome to borrow it."

"Thanks anyway, but I'm already sweating like a hog. I sure don't need a jacket."

"That's precisely why you do need a jacket. You hav'ta keep your body temperature stable. You let your pitchin' arm cool down too fast and it will get as stiff as taffy. We both know, a stiff arm is just beggin' for an injury. Remember, ya gotta baby your jelly joints."

"It doesn't seem like my arm could cool down much today. I'll bet it's 90 degrees in the shade."

"It's not that warm, but even if it were, you'd need to cover at least *that* arm. As a pitcher, that arm is your #1 business asset. Ruin it and you'll put yourself out of business. Is that what you want?"

"Heck, no!"

Mr. Bloomstack suddenly changed his tone of voice and manner of speaking. Dan knew he used that voice only when he was dead serious. "Dan, think of a nylon jacket as insuring that asset. Let me put this into perspective for you. You've invested a lot of your time and energy in becoming the best pitcher you can be. If you injure that arm, you could lose your entire investment."

Dan got the picture. He retrieved Mr. Bloomstack's jacket from the hook next to the freezer door. He slipped his pitching arm into the sleeve. As he headed back outside he caught his reflection in the glass of a framed baseball poster. He looked weird. The right sleeve, with a large black and white #72, hung below his knees, and the other one was dangling on the ground.

"I hope no one sees me lookin' like this," Dan complained as he rejoined Mr. Bloomstack.

"I've got a couple of things to say about that, too. First, you look like a smart ball player, and second," Mr. Bloomstack fell back into his slang talk, "you're wastin' your mental resources thinkin' about what other people might think of you. Most of the time they're too busy thinkin' about themselves to give you much notice. Get it?"

"Got it."

"Good." They sat in the shade finishing their lemonade. Mr. Bloomstack talked about the legends of the early years of baseball—guys like Babe Ruth and Hank Greenberg. Ralph Bloomstack could talk baseball and tell baseball stories for hours on end. He studied Dan's handiwork on the pitching wall. "That's a pretty good lookin' strike zone you've made there. You realize that in a real game the size of that zone will change depending upon the batter."

"Sure, it's always below the batter's arm pits and the bottom of his knees."

"Right, a good batter will crouch to reduce his strike zone. Did I ever tell you the story of Eddie Gaedel?"

"Nope!" Dan responded enthusiastically.

A wide smile came across Mr. Bloomstack's face. "There's a great story about Bill Veeck when he was the general of the St. Louis Browns. Bill was a great showman, and liked to play practical jokes. He signed up the famous midget Eddie Gaedel, who was only 3 feet, 7 inches, and sent him in to bat. When Eddie crouched, he could create about a three-inch strike zone. Can you believe it? Three measly inches."

The near impossibility of getting a strike under those conditions had Dan laughing until tears ran down his cheeks.

Mr. Bloomstack tousled Dan's hair and continued. "Man, I'd have loved to have been there to throw some raspberries."

"Sounds like a waste of good raspberries to me," Dan chuckled.

"You pullin' my leg boy? You know throwin' raspberries means hecklin' a player, right?"

Dan just smiled. They sat each thinking their separate thoughts for a couple of minutes.

Then Mr. Bloomstack asked, "How's Wall doin' as an umpire?"

"Better than I'm doin' as a pitcher."

"Nobody's expectin' you to be perfect. But if you pay attention to what Wall tells you, I guarantee you'll see a little bit of improvement every day."

"That's what Coach Tisdale calls kaizen."

"Kaizen. Never heard that word before." He pulled a small palm pilot from his pocket. "How do you spell that?"

Dan was surprised. Mr. Bloomstack was more with it than he had imagined. "I don't know. I can ask Coach at practice tomorrow."

"I'll key it in phonetically until you get back to me."

Dan watched him key in the information. He hadn't thought of Mr. Bloomstack as someone who would be interested in new words. He didn't seem to treat the ones he already knew with much respect.

Dan studied Mr. Bloomstack. With a slight hesitation he asked, "Mr. B, since you like baseball so much, why is it you don't play on one of the teams in the Men's League?"

Mr. Bloomstack put his left hand across his mouth and moved it back and forth. He lowered his head and seemed to look through his eyebrows at Dan. "I didn't mind my business."

Dan stiffened. He had crossed a line without intending to. He hadn't meant to be nosy, or had he? He really did want to know why Mr. Bloomstack didn't pitch anymore. He also knew it wasn't any of his business. He had let curiosity get the best of him, and he wasn't sure what to say now.

Mr. Bloomstack picked up on Dan's embarrassment. His voice was soft and serious. "What I mean by 'I didn't mind my business', Dan, is that I didn't protect my assets as well as I should have. I was good and knew I was good. I felt invincible. The press built me up, and I believed everything they wrote. I was terrific. I was a natural. Well ..., maybe I was ..., maybe I wasn't."

Mr. Bloomstack sat with his elbows on his knees and looked out across the empty baseball diamond. "I started to goof off. I took it a little too easy the summer before I headed off to college. Hung around with the gang. I figured I could slack off and still outshine everyone else. I didn't see any sense in being the best I could be. I figured I only had to be better than the competition. The trouble was, I had no idea that when I got to college, I was going to find a whole new level of competition."

Mr. Bloomstack straightened up and looked at Dan with very sad eyes. "The first day of freshman practice, I could see I wasn't as special as I thought I was. I was going to have some strong competition for starting pitcher. Not from one guy, but from two. I started pushing myself. Trying to play catch-up from a summer of goofing off. Trying to get my arm back in top shape before the coach posted his starting roster."

Dan listened intently. Mr. Bloomstack crossed his arms, and rocked back and forth a couple of times. Then he sat absolutely still and continued, "It happened only a couple of days before the first game of the season. I was warming up. Out of the corner of my eye I saw the coaching team standing outside the bullpen watching me. I decided to show them just what I could do. I hadn't completed my warm-up, but figured they might not still be standing there by the time I had.

"I made a couple of hotshot pitches. I was all smiles inside. On my third pitch I heard a pop, felt a snap like the release of a rubber band and a strong pain. I was a macho type back then, so I toughed it out. I pitched another half-dozen pitches. By then it wasn't a pretty picture. My arm was shaking uncontrollably. I couldn't even grasp the ball with my right hand. The doctor said I had torn the medial collateral ligament in my pitching arm. That was it. I had burnt my major asset. I was out of business."

"If it was a ligament couldn't they do something, an operation or something?" Dan asked.

Mr. Bloomstack nodded in the affirmative. "Today they could. They'd give me a 'Tommy John'. They'd replace my torn tendon with a strong tendon from my left arm."

"Sounds ugly," Dan said.

"I'm sure it is, but they say it's usually effective. The doc drills holes in the bones above and below the elbow, and then threads the strong tendon from your non-pitching arm through those holes as neat as you please, but that operation wasn't around in my day."

They sat quietly looking out at the empty playing fields for some time, then Mr. Bloomstack gave a tug to the sleeve of #72. "You just make sure, Mr. Dan Martin, that you always know the true value of all your assets, and make doubly sure you protect them and use them well."

Dan bit his lower lip and nodded. They sat side by side, yet each was alone. Dan glanced at Mr. Bloomstack a couple of times. Each time, the intense sadness he saw and somehow felt responsible for made him look away.

CHAPTER FIFTEEN
THE WHISPER

The next day, things were back to normal. Dan arrived early at the concession stand so he would have plenty of time for a good workout with Wall. Mr. Bloomstack swiveled his chair away from his computer to get a better view through the screen door of Dan's technique. After watching a half-dozen pitches he got up and went outside. "How would you like to meet another one of my friends?"

"One of your coaching friends?"

"Yeah, you might say that."

"Any friend of yours is a friend of mine, Mr. B."

"I think you could work on your hand speed." With the grace of a magician, Mr. Bloomstack pulled out the towel that always dangled from his pocket when he was working around the concession stand. "My friend, Towel here, may be of some assistance to you."

Dan laughed. "You have some pretty strange friends, Mr. B."

"Strange perhaps, but very helpful. You'll want to keep your glove for this drill, just for the feel of it, but you won't need a ball."

"Drill? That sounds wicked." Dan's eyes widened in anticipation.

"It's wicked all right. When you do this drill right, Towel here will whisper in your ear. If he's not whispering to you, you haven't solved your problem."

"Com'on, Mr. B, no towel's gonna whisper to me. I wasn't born yesterday."

"Call it what you want, but when you get the proper arm action, you'll see your hand speed improve, and you'll hear a 'whipping' action from Towel here. Get it?"

Dan smiled. "So what's the drill?"

"Scrunch one end of Towel up until he feels about the size of your baseball. Then hold that wad just like a ball you're about to pitch. Notice Towel still has a nice long tail dangling down. How does that feel?"

"Not much like a baseball. It's too soft and too light."

"That's okay, you'll get used to it. I'm gonna stand right here just out of arm's reach. You're gonna pretend to pitch to me, but keep a firm grip on Towel; don't release him. Spread your feet apart a comfortable delivery stance. Good, your back foot has a nice perpendicular line to me. Straighten your front foot a smidgen so it's pointing straight at me with your knee inside the foot. Perfect. Does that feel comfortable?"

"Pretty much."

"Level your shoulders now," Mr. Bloomstack instructed. Dan immediately adjusted his shoulders. "Lookin' good. Your shoulder on your glove side is pointed right at me, just like it should be. How's your weight feel?"

"I'm pretty evenly balanced. How should I be?"

"As you are, just as you are. Keep your head and your eyes level looking straight at me. I'm your target."

"Target? You mean you want me to slap you with this towel?"

Mr. Bloomstack stepped aside. "Let's see you throw a pitch."

Dan pivoted on his back foot and completed a throwing motion.

"I'll stand right here," Mr. Bloomstack said, as he moved back in front of Dan, but a bit further back than he previously had been. He crouched down on one knee in a catcher position, placed his elbow on his knee, and held his glove in an open palm position. "Okay now. When you've fully extended your pitch, Towel should hit my glove. When I say pitch, you execute, savvy? Remember to listen for Towel's whisper.... Pitch!"

Dan pitched, but there was no whisper, just a slap when Towel hit Mr. Bloomstack's glove.

"Pitch. Pitch. Pitch. You're doin' great with your legs and the trunk of your body, but you're shifting your head. Keep your head still.... Pitch.... That's better."

"Towel's not whispering."

"He will. It may take a little time. Your head's good now, but it looks like your arm's a might bit stiff. Towel insists on nice jelly joints. He won't whisper for a stiff arm. Pitch. Pitch. Pitch."

"It feels like I'm doin' everything right, but there's no whisperin'," Dan complained. He was getting frustrated. This wasn't fun anymore.

"Okay, move around and get some of the tension out of your body. You're tryin' too hard. Relax. Rotate your shoulders first clockwise and then counterclockwise. Now do the same thing, only slant your shoulders and do only one shoulder at a time. Lookin' good. Let's try it again. Pitch.... Pitch."

"I heard it!" Dan shouted. "Towel whispered."

Mr. Bloomstack just smiled. "Pitch. Pitch. Pitch. Pitch."

"Towel's stopped whisperin'."

Mr. Bloomstack stood up and stretched. "Is your arm feeling a bit tight?"

"I don't know, maybe."

"Just remember, when Towel whispers you're doin' it right. That's enough for today. Five minutes a day with Towel is plenty. Tomorrow you can do this drill with Wall. I'm a little old for this crouchin' stuff."

"But Wall won't be able to tell me how to make corrections in my delivery," Dan complained.

"That's true. But when you get it right, Towel will whisper. One word of caution. If Towel isn't whispering after a dozen deliveries, you need to lay off, and do something else for a while."

"A dozen deliveries, that's not much. How can I ever get it right if that's all I do?" Dan said irritably.

"Here's a little secret. Drills create muscle memory. It's extremely important that drills be done correctly. If they aren't, the muscle memory you'll be teaching your body will just be a bad habit. Let me tell you from experience, bad habits can be very hard to break. When the time comes that Towel is whispering to you regularly, then you can practice a longer time."

"Don't you want to stay with me until Towel whispers regular?"

"Not necessary. You're the one who has to concentrate on what you're doin'. We've walked through the drill together. You've heard Towel whisper. You know the results you need."

"But I'm doin' it wrong more than I'm doin' it right. I think we should practice together again tomorrow."

"You'll see. Towel will start to whisper to you, and you'll develop good muscle memory and your movements will become automatic. You won't even have to think about it. That will free your mind to think about the parts of the game that aren't routine. If you haven't mastered it after a couple of days, let me know, and we'll start again from the beginning." With that Mr. Bloomstack turned and walked toward the concession stand.

"It's a deal," Dan said, but his thoughts were very different: "He's always walkin' away before we finish something. He's always expectin' me to reason things out, when I don't know the first thing about it. He's just like Grant, always naggin' me to think. Think, think, think. I'm tired of thinkin'. Think at school, think at work, and now it's think about makin' a stupid towel whisper. What was it with these guys anyway? Always sayin' crap like, 'Practice makes perfect' or 'The way you practice is the way you'll play the game' or 'Be the best you can be.' Why won't people just leave me alone?"

The next afternoon Dan was still in a snit. Towel would only whisper randomly. He couldn't figure out just what he was doing wrong. He muttered his discontent as he roughly loaded the bottles into the pop machine, not caring if a bottle might break.

When he finished he tossed the empty box across the room, knocking the potato chip rack to the floor near where Mr. Bloomstack was talking on the phone. Mr. Bloomstack raised an eyebrow, and looked at Dan over his glasses, but there was no break in his conversation.

Dan listened in annoyance. Mr. Bloomstack was talking in one of his different voices, and his accent sounded like he was playing some character in a movie. Dan normally enjoyed Mr. Bloomstack's different voices, but today he was feeling angry, and he directed his anger at Mr. Bloomstack as soon as he was off the phone. "Why is it you talk in those dumb voices?" Dan challenged.

"How's that?"

"Well, like just now on the phone. You had an accent of some kind."

"Wha'da'ya mean?"

"Wha'da'ya mean, wha'da'ya mean?" Dan voice was accusatory.

Sally Bloomstack, who had been sitting in the corner reading a paper, laughed. "Dan's picked up on your 'mirroring,' Ralph."

"His what?" Dan asked.

"Mirroring, you know, he sometimes talks and acts like the person he's talking to. It's like Ralph is a mirror. You cross your arms, he crosses his arms. You lean forward, he leans forward. You accent a word a certain way, and he does the same." She turned toward her husband. "They call that mirroring, don't they?"

Mr. Bloomstack nodded. "Ah, ha. Well, Mr. Dan Martin, I admit it, I do sometimes talk differently. Been doin' that since I was in grade school. Not even aware I'm doin' it most of the time."

"How can you not be aware you're doin' it?" Dan questioned.

"It just happens, kinda automatic. Guess it's like one of your muscle memories."

"My muscle memories aren't doing too well right now, thanks to you."

Mr. Bloomstack chose not to hear that, and continued. "I've trained my language."

Dan felt like saying his language could use a lot more training, but instead he demanded, "How's that?"

"When I was in the sixth grade, this kid from the South moved to Stewart. His name was Jimmy John. He had a really strange accent. Half the time, we kids weren't sure what he was sayin'. We were always teasin' and makin' fun of him. None of us wanted anything to do with a guy who couldn't even talk right."

Dan got caught up in Mr. Bloomstack's story. "Yeah, I know what you mean. There was a girl from Scotland that visited the McGladry's next door. Grant liked her, thought she was real pretty. But she'd have to say somethin' five or six times before I could understand what she was sayin'. She sounded weird."

"You're sure she was the one that sounded weird?" Mr. Bloomstack looked at Dan through his eyebrows, the look that Dan could now recognize as the 'I'm about to set you straight' look. Mr. Bloomstack continued. "One day my old man heard me and my friends makin' fun of Jimmy John. When my friends left, Dad gave me quite a talkin' to, told me that it was probably just as hard for Jimmy John to understand me as it was for me to understand him. He said I needed to give some consideration to learnin' Jimmy John's language, and if I did that, I'd probably find out he was a pretty nice fellow."

Dan was confused. "I thought you said this Jimmy John guy was from the South. They speak English in the South, don't they?"

"That's just what I told my dad. He said there's more than one way to speak English, and sometimes an accent can almost sound like a different language."

"Your dad was sure right. That Scottish girl sure sounded like she was speakin' a foreign language."

Mr. Bloomstack smiled. "Then my dad said, that if Jimmy John and I truly spoke the same language we wouldn't be havin' any difficulty understanding one another. He told me to start listenin' carefully to Jimmy John, and when I talked to him, I should try and talk his language."

"That's rude; I'll bet Jimmy John slugged you for makin' fun of him, right?"

"Nope, as a matter of fact he told me he really liked hangin' out with me, because I was the only guy at school that didn't talk with a funny accent."

"So?" Dan challenged.

"So Jimmy John and I moved past the language barrier. You have to learn to knock certain barriers aside, if you want to get on down the road to what's really important. If I want people to hear what I'm saying, truly hear me, I don't want them struggling to understand my words, or feeling uncomfortable with how I act. I want them listenin' to what I say. The more I talk and act like them, the less distracted they'll be, and then we can both concentrate on the important business at hand, whatever that might be."

Dan studied Mr. Bloomstack. Maybe the old guy had more respect for words than Dan thought. He remembered the time Mr. Bloomstack asked about the word 'kaizen,' and then there were the big words he sometimes used on the telephone. Yet, there was something about this whole thing that seemed a bit deceitful, not quite right. He just couldn't put his finger on it.

Mr. Bloomstack saw the disapproval on Dan's face. "You can train yourself to listen to the nuances of language just like you train yourself to recognize the nuances of different pitchers, and different pitching styles. For example, how many forms of English do you already speak?"

"I only speak English-English."

"Are you tellin' me you talk the same way to your teacher as you do to your buddies when you're alone?"

"Heck no, I'd get sent to the principal's office."

"Do you talk the same way to someone you've just met as you do to friends, or do you talk the same way to Grant as you do your mom?"

Dan smiled. "It's the same English, it's just some of the words are different."

"I'll bet you dollars to donuts it's not even the same English. Unless things have changed since I went to school. I'd guess you aren't droppin' your final g's in front of your teachers. And what about the 'nah's' and the 'yeah's'?" Mr. Bloomstack challenged.

"That's a different situation."

"My point exactly. When in Rome you do as the Romans do. Think situation specific. So, if I'm ... *talkin'* ... your language, I'm ... *gonna'* ... talk the same as you do. *D'ya* ... see what I mean?"

Dan laughed. "Does that mean if I don't drop my g's, you won't either?"

"Try me and see."

Dan's mood had changed completely. He stood up and gave Mr. Bloomstack a friendly slap on the shoulder. "You're a character, Mr. B. How about a contest? The first one to drop a final 'g' has to load the pop machine for the next week."

Sally Bloomstack put her paper down. "I'm appointing myself umpire," she said, "and I'm going to insist on a handicap for Dan. Ralph, you've had decades of practice. I think Dan needs a minimum of a three errors."

"Come on, Sally, there are no handicaps in baseball," Mr. Bloomstack joked.

"This isn't baseball," Mrs. Bloomstack countered.

"Are you saying it's one strike and I'm out, but Dan gets three strikes? That doesn't seem entirely fair and square," Mr. Bloomstack challenged.

"You're absolutely right, Ralph. That's not entirely fair. I'll make it six errors for Dan." With that she picked up her paper and appeared to read.

"Well, you heard the umpire." Mr. Bloomstack slapped the table and stood up. "When do you want to start?"

"How about right now?"

"You're on."

Dan flung out his arms, and twirled in a circle to energize himself for the challenge. As he did so, he knocked Mr. Bloomstack's warm-up jacket from its peg. "Sorry," Dan said as he casually picked up the jacket, brushed it off, and hung it back on the hook.

Mr. Bloomstack went over and hung the jacket so that the #72 on the sleeve was showing. "You know why that #72 is so important?"

"Sure, that was your number when you played for Roosevelt. Everyone knows that," Dan answered matter-of-factly.

"You've got it cattywampus. It's because the #72 is important that I always asked to have it on my uniforms. It's sort of my own personal talisman."

"What's a talisman?" Dan asked.

"That's for me to know and for you to find out."

Mrs. Bloomstack shook her head. "Honestly, Ralph, don't be such a tease."

"I'm not teasing; I'm encouraging Dan to do some research."

"Hmm!" Mrs. Bloomstack gave him a look and went back to her reading.

"Okay, maybe I was teasing a bit," Mr. Bloomstack shrugged and added, "A talisman is something people believe has magical powers. A sort of charm."

"Wow! Is that why you were so good? I'm gonna ask Coach Tisdale for #72 first thing tomorrow."

"I think I just heard strike one. What are you *going* to do tomorrow?"

Dan clinched his teeth. "Darn, I'm *going* to ask Coach Tisdale for #72 first thing tomorrow."

"Hold on, it's only magic if you're playing the money game. It won't help you a tinker's dollar for baseball."

Dan had no idea what a tinker's dollar was. Maybe it was magic too, but he wasn't going let Mr. Bloomstack sidetrack him. "So how's this 72 magic thing work? Do I need to rub it or say special words?"

"Nope, the magic is all in helping you decide how to spend your money."

"I don't need magic for that. It's real easy to spend my money."

"Well, the more you know about the money game, the harder you may find it is to spend it."

"That doesn't make sense. The whole purpose of money is to spend it. Right?"

"Right, the whole purpose of money is to spend it. But how you spend it determines if you're a loser or a winner.

If you understand the magic of 72, you increase your chances of becoming a winner."

Dan fidgeted. "So, you gonna tell me the secret?"

"I might, but I think I just heard a strike. That's two down and four to go." Mr. Bloomstack gleefully rubbed his palms together. "About the magic of 72—you bring me a list of everything you spend your money on for a week, and I'll share the secret of 72 with you. Is it a deal?"

Dan thought carefully about his words before he answered. "You better believe it!" Dan high-fived Mr. Bloomstack, picked up the carton he had thrown earlier, and righted the potato chips display rack. He was in a good mood again, and figured it had to be easier to keep track of the money he spent for a week than to make Towel whisper.

CHAPTER SIXTEEN
POWER OF 72

"There's the man," Mr. Bloomstack greeted Dan. "I have been meaning to tell you, you're looking mighty good on the mound. Nice arm extension, and good hand speed. It looks like old Towel has been doing a good job of coaching you."

"Thanks Mr. B, but I have to admit there were times when I felt like stuffing old Towel in the trash can."

"I can understand that. I remember there were times I dreaded seeing my coach walk toward me carrying a towel. Particularly when it was to correct an over-stride problem I had. He would put the towel out in front of me at the appropriate distance, and if my stride was too long, my foot would land on the towel. It took me forever to correct that problem. My muscle memory had locked into an over-stride, and retraining those muscles wasn't easy. I would get so mad at Coach for not just telling me how to do it correctly."

"Tell me about it. It would have been a lot quicker and a whole lot easier if you had just told me what to do to correct my hand speed," Dan complained.

"True, but you wouldn't have learned as much, and that certainly wouldn't have respected your abilities. This way, you have been your own problem solver. You've learned to make self-corrections."

"I guess, but it's a pain."

"No pain, no gain, as they say."

"Not another saying?"

Mr. Bloomstack patted Dan on the head. "When you're on the mound, the only coach you have access to is the one in your head. You have to learn to coach yourself. Remember, the way you practice is the way you'll play."

Dan rolled his eyes. "You forgot 'Practice makes perfect,' and 'Be the best you can be,'" Dan mocked.

"Glad you remembered," Mr. Bloomstack said cheerily, purposely ignoring Dan's tone of voice.

Dan shrugged. It was clear he wasn't going to get any sympathy, so he decided to change the subject. "Do you have any other strange friends I should know about?"

"I became pretty good friends with a paper cup, also."

"So just what does Mr. Cup do?"

"Old Cup helped me with my push-off leg. Coach would set Cup about two feet to the right of my push-off foot and a few inches toward home plate. The trick was to have my push-off foot circle over the cup to help me complete my throw with the least amount of stress."

"Can't imagine you stressed, Mr. B., but my push-offs are near perfect. Miss Hutchinson has really helped me there. She doesn't expect me to coach myself. During my ballet lesson she watches every little movement and immediately corrects my form to make sure it's perfect."

"Well, well, well. I wondered when you were going to tell me about your ballet classes."

Dan got defensive. "The classes help me with my pitching. I'm not the only one. Some of the varsity guys take ballet lessons too. How'd you know about it?"

"There's not much that goes on in this town I don't know about. I also know you've been taking flack from Gabby and Spider about it."

"Yeah, well, they just don't get it, but Chandler is thinking about signing on."

"Good for him, and good for you. I'm glad you have the confidence to stick with it. I wish I had a dime for every person who lets their friends discourage them from taking the path to success."

"You sound like my dad. He used to say he wished he had a dime for every guy who took the wrong path just because that was the path his friends were taking."

"Your dad was a wise man."

Dan nodded. Mr. Bloomstack could see from Dan's eyes that he was on an inward journey. He sat quietly waiting for Dan to return. It didn't take long, just a minute or two at the most.

"Mr. B., you seem to want me to explore and to learn to coach myself. Miss Hutchinson gives no room for exploration. You can't both be right."

"Here's the deal." Mr. Bloomstack checked Dan's eyes to make sure he was still with him. "You have a lot of coaches. We all have different styles. Madeline is good at what she does. Carlsen is good at what he does. Grant is good at what he does. I'm good at what I do. We each are trying to teach you different things. It doesn't make any difference if our teaching styles are different as long as the results we are after aren't in conflict."

He paused, "But, hear this. Coach Tisdale is your head coach. He has the final word. You need to keep him informed about all training you're doing when he's not around."

"I guess there is no conflict in results; it's just your teaching styles are so-o-o-o different."

"That's not a problem. That just adds spice to life."

Dan picked up three cups from the counter and began to juggle them.

"Can you do that if they're full of water?"

"Sure," Dan laughed, "but you wouldn't want to be standin' too close by."

"What's that? What's that? Did my ears miss something? Did you perhaps drop a 'g'?"

Dan groaned. He bent over and pretended to scoop up the fallen 'g' from the floor and shove it in his mouth. "You wouldn't want to be *standing* too close by," he repeated. Dan had learned to quickly correct his language and move on.

Unfortunately, this latest slip up had brought Dan's total to five errors. The contest was down to the wire. If either one of them dropped a 'g' the other would be loading the pop machine for a week.

Dan initially had thought he could win by just not talking when he was around Mr. Bloomstack, but he found that was much harder to do than he had imagined. It seemed to work best to just keep his words on the forefront of his mind. Dan reached over, picked up his backpack from the floor, and plopped it on the table. "I have my list of how I spent my money. I'm ready for the secret of 72 whenever you have time, Mr. B."

"Kept good records, have you?"

"Yes, sir." Every night before going to bed, Dan had written down every penny he had spent during that day. He pulled out his list of expenditures.

"The first thing you have to do is to total up every penny you spent for the entire week."

"I've already done that. I spent $10.23."

"Keeping ahead of the old man, are you? I like that. Okay, the next thing you do is separate your 'needs' from your 'wants'. Put an 'N' next to items you really truly needed. From here it looks like all your expenditures were wants."

Dan frowned. "Are you reading my list upside down?"

"Absolutely."

"That's not fair."

"If life were fair, horses would ride people half the time. Besides, where's the rule book that says I can't get information by reading upside down, sideways, with mirrors, or even with the eyes in the back of my head, for that matter?"

Dan turned his list over and slid it under his backpack. "It's cheating. I didn't say you could look at my list."

"If you didn't want me to see your list, you shouldn't have given me the opportunity. Plain and simple."

"Just because you had the opportunity didn't mean you had to take it."

"Every game I've ever played has always been about skill and opportunity. Don't you take every opportunity to study the technique of every pitcher you see?"

Dan nodded.

Mr. Bloomstack continued. "When was the last time one of those pitchers gave you permission to study their technique?"

Dan looked chagrined.

"Well," Mr. Bloomstack tapped his finger on the table. "I've learned reading upside down gives me certain advantages in playing the money game. There's no law against it. It's a fair-and-square technique and it comes in handy now and then. I'll bet you dollars to donuts I'm not the first one to read one of your papers upside down. Every teacher I know does it. Now are you going to harp on my reading upside down all morning, or are we going to get on with the magic of 72?"

Dan shrugged and pulled his list out from under his backpack. "Get on with it."

"Good. To make the magic of 72 work for you, you'll have to be very honest about what is truly a 'need' and what is truly a 'want.' Just how is a movie a need, and what about all those pizzas and sodas?" Mr. Bloomstack asked.

"All the guys decided to go to the movies so I had to go too, and in the summer we always go to Jimmy's after the ball games. I can't just occupy a seat. I have to buy something."

"Well now, I can see why you might *want* to go to a movie, and why you might *want* to go to Jimmy's after a ball game, but I'm not sure you *needed* to do either one."

Dan looked at his list a second time, and then a third, and finally said, "I guess all of my expenditures were wants."

"Good, it's important to be honest with yourself. Now go through your list and circle everything you would be willing to buy at twice the price."

"I wouldn't buy any of them at twice the price. I'm not stupid."

"Well, that is in effect what you do every time you buy a 'want.' You make a choice to pay the hidden cost."

"I never paid twice the price for any of them. I paid the same as everyone else," Dan countered defensively.

"Oh, you paid it, you just didn't know it. I said it was hidden."

"How could I pay something and not know it?"

"What you paid was an opportunity cost. Every dollar you spend today means you lost the opportunity to put that dollar to work to make additional future dollars."

"You're talking compound interest again, right?"

"Right, and the magic of 72 is the lightning-speed way to see exactly how long it will take you to double your money. You don't even need a calculator. You can do it in your head. All you have to do is take the interest rate and divide it into 72. And voila! That's how long it will take you to double your money. Neat, huh?"

"You mean if the interest rate is 6 percent, it would take 12 years to double my money?"

"Right!"

"Twelve years is forever; it's most of my lifetime. I'd rather spend the money now."

"Okay, look at it this way. If you spend $2.75 a day that you didn't need to spend, that's $1,000 a year gone forever. But if you instead saved the money and invested it at only 6 percent interest, it would double in just 12 years. Just think how much money that would come to by the time you're my age."

"I'd like that kind of money, but my friends are worth more than money. I have to go to the movies and Jimmy's."

"What makes you think that Gabby, Chandler, and Spider wouldn't want to know about the power of 72?"

Mr. Bloomstack reached into his pocket and pulled out a penny, flipped it on the floor and walked away.

"Okay, okay, I'll think on it," Dan called after him.

Mr. Bloomstack stuck his head back into the room. "You do that. I didn't say it was easy. It never is. It was tough for me as a kid." He paused. "It's still tough sometimes. That's why I need the #72 to remind me. It keeps me focused on the hidden cost. That way, every 'want' I buy makes me feel great, 'cause for me it really is worth twice the price."

Dan leaned over and picked up the penny from the floor. He put it in his pocket and followed Mr. Bloomstack into the service area of the concession stand.

"Mr. B, what kind of *want* is worth twice the price for you?"

"Guess it comes down to one of two things. Either it's a good investment, or it's something that I'm passionate about."

"Like what?"

Mr. Bloomstack gave Dan a wink. "Like a new toy."

"Come on Mr. B, for real."

"Like I said, a new toy. Just because I have gray hair doesn't mean I don't play with toys."

"You're kidding me, right?"

Mrs. Bloomstack looked up from her work. "I've never seen a grown man with so many toys."

Mr. Bloomstack smiled. "Now Sally, some of them have turned out to be pretty good investments."

"Perhaps, but you didn't buy them as an investment, and you'll have to sell them to realize a gain. I can't remember the last time you sold one of your toys."

"But if I needed to sell them I could." Mr. Bloomstack turned toward Dan. "Would you like to see my toys, Mr. Dan Martin? That is, if Sally says it's okay."

Mrs. Bloomstack raised an eyebrow. "Well Dan, I can see you're very special. Ralph doesn't normally play with his toys on work days. He's just like a kid when he gets up in his clubhouse. Sometimes he even misses his meals. I'm trusting you to get him back down here in an hour."

"Yes, ma'am."

Mr. Bloomstack gave Sally a kiss on the cheek. Then he put his hand on Dan's shoulder and steered him into the back room. They walked up to the metal shelf unit that held paper products. Mr. Bloomstack pushed aside a roll of paper towels to expose something that looked like a mirror. He put his right hand on the mirror, and the entire wall, along with the metal shelf, swung inward. A wide hidden staircase appeared.

CHAPTER SEVENTEEN
CRYSTAL CLEAR

"Open, says me." Mr. Bloomstack chuckled at his own play on words. Taking the steps two at a time he called over his shoulder, "Don't just stand there gawking. Come on up."

Dan didn't move. He stood wide-eyed on the threshold of the secret staircase. Mrs. Bloomstack leaned against the doorframe to the service area. "Ralph's full of surprises, isn't he, Dan?"

"I've worked here for weeks and didn't even know about this secret staircase."

"Well, you haven't seen the half of it. Remember now," she reminded him, "one hour."

Dan stepped cautiously through the doorway. On the wall at the foot of the staircase was a photo of Ted Williams with an arm around Mr. Bloomstack's shoulder. The photo was signed, "To a champion collector and a good friend, Ted." Dan studied the picture, and then shouted up the stairwell, "WOW! Mr. B, I didn't know you were old enough to know Ted Williams."

"You're only as old as you think you are, and if you're gonna look at every little thing, you'll be an old man yourself before you get up here."

"Strike!" Dan yelled jubilantly. He had won. The adrenaline flowed and he bounded up the stairs, only glancing at the mementos that lined both sides of the stairwell. "You load the pop machine for the next ..." He stopped in mid-sentence and stood wide-eyed, trying to take everything in.

The huge room appeared to be a combination skybox, entertainment center, library, and museum. Mr. Bloomstack was settled into a big easy chair with his back to Dan. He was facing a gigantic computer screen, apparently surfing the web from his desktop media center. Dan looked past him toward two walls of tall bookcases that held books, notebooks, CDs, DVDs, and video tapes. Baseball paraphernalia covered the top of every bookcase and even hung from the ceiling.

Mr. Bloomstack swirled his chair and enjoyed the moment of Dan's awe. "As you were saying?"

Dan didn't hear him. He was still trying to process his surroundings. To his right was a wall of drawers and three racks of baseball bats, with 20 wooden bats in each rack. Dan was fascinated by many odd shapes he had never seen, such as a flat bat, a spring bat, and a mushroom bat. There was an entire rack of special edition Louisville Sluggers. One was a century old. Several had names either stamped or burnt into them. Dan stood before one of the bat racks and ran his finger across the stamped names of Joe Jackson, Ty Cobb, Lou Gehrig, Jackie Robinson, Mickey Mantle, and several with George "Babe" Ruth. One bat had been cracked and then repaired with a whole bunch of small steel brads. There was another rack of bats with decal labels. One of them, a Spalding Black Betsy, was particularly beautiful, long, sleek, and black. Dan imagined himself swinging it.

He turned to see his reflection in a wall of windows that overlooked Diamond 1. Under the window was a bench made entirely of bats and baseballs. He shook his head in disbelief. The other wall was lined with glass-front cases holding antique balls, mitts, catcher's masks, bases, and such. On top of the cases were all sorts of baseball board games, banks, trophies, and statues. The center of the room was occupied with an oversized library table surrounded by desk chairs. Two manikins, one in a Red Sox uniform and the other in a Yankee uniform, were sitting in two of the chairs. At the end of the table nearest Dan was a glass-topped case with World Series rings. Each had the name of a player engraved on the inside. The place of honor held a Willie Mays ring. At the far end of the table was a crystal pedestal that held a glistening crystal baseball. Dan had never imagined anything like this, not even in his most creative daydreams.

"Well, what do you think?" Mr. Bloomstack asked.

Dan just stared into the crystal baseball. Mr. Bloomstack tapped his knuckles on the table. "What do you think?" he asked again.

Dan finally logged in. "WOW! Mr. B, this is amazing. Is that a real crystal ball?"

"Glad to see you're back online. It's a real crystal baseball, alright."

"Does it tell the future?"

"No, it doesn't forecast the future, but it will help you keep the future in mind. Isn't it a beauty? That's one of my favorite toys. It's a little like the #72. That crystal baseball holds one of the secrets of success for those in the know."

"What do I have to do to learn the secret?"

"I already told you the secret; it helps you keep the future in mind."

"How so?"

"I know a coach that gives every player a crystal baseball when they first join his team. It's a reminder that their reputation is as fragile as a crystal ball, and just as easily damaged. He wants them to remember that their conduct is always under their control, *on* or *off* the field."

"That sounds just like Coach Tisdale. He's always talking about good conduct on or off the field."

"Right. Coaches don't want you to drop the ball or hang around with people who do. Your reputation could shatter just like a crystal ball that has been dropped. Even if you pick up all the pieces and work hard to mend your reputation, it will never be the same. The flaw will always be visible."

Dan lowered his head, squinted, and tried to look through his eyebrows just as he had seen Mr. Bloomstack do many times. "That's just a fairy tale. You can't play the game without dropping the ball."

Mr. Bloomstack recognized he was being mirrored, and worked to hold back a smile. "It's not unusual to have the ball pop out of your glove, but once it's in your bare hand you have good control over it."

Mr. Bloomstack picked up a ball from a group that was on a table next to his chair and handed it to Dan. "See what I mean? Once it's firm in your hand you're not going to drop the ball unless you're either careless or it's deliberate."

"I have to *hand* it to you Mr. B; you can sure make things crystal clear."

"That's pretty good. Did you intend that pun?"

"Me? I just meant you made your case, *handily*."

Mr. Bloomstack hesitated only a second before responding, "That's good, because I want you to understand this crystal baseball concept like the *back of your hand*."

Dan smiled; this was almost as good as a game of burn-out. "Appreciate that, Mr. B. I'm sure all this 'on the field' 'off the field' stuff will come in *mighty handy.*"

"You know me; I'm always pleased to offer a *helping hand.*" Mr. Bloomstack pointed his index finger at Dan to indicate it was now his turn.

Dan did a little hip-hop dance. He was really enjoying the game. "All you have to do is admit I've won, *hands down.*" He spun around full circle and pointed to Mr. Bloomstack.

There was no response for quite a while; then finally Mr. Bloomstack said, "You're quite a *handful,* Mr. Dan Martin, but you need to be careful not to *overplay your hand.*"

Dan groaned hearing a double pun; he knew that meant he'd have to send a double back. He started to moonwalk around the conference table, trying to buy time as his mind tried to think of more "hand" puns. Almost a minute went by before Dan formulated a response. "If you feel I have the *upper hand*, or that this game is *getting out of hand*, you can always *throw up your hands* and declare me the winner."

"It's pretty clear I have *my hands full* when I try playing a word game with you," Mr. Bloomstack conceded.

"That's only a single; you have to match my triple."

Mr. Bloomstack rolled his eyes toward the ceiling, threw his hands up in the air, and let out an exaggerated gasp of defeat.

"Yes!" Dan shouted, and delivered an energetic high five to each of Mr. Bloomstack's raised hands.

"Bottom line, do you understand the significance of the crystal baseball?" Mr. Bloomstack asked.

"I understand the symbolism, but everyone makes mistakes."

"Honest mistakes don't count. They're the ones you don't know you're making. With an honest mistake, it's like you're still playing in a sandlot. A crystal ball won't break if it falls on sand."

"You mean like making fun of the way Jimmy Jack talked, before your dad straightened you out?"

"That's a good example. If I had continued to make fun of Jimmy Jack, I couldn't claim ignorance; I would have been guilty of willful poor judgment. I'd have dropped the ball. It might not break. Maybe the crack would be so small that I would be the only one to know it's there, but if there were a lot of small cracks, my crystal ball would look cloudy to anyone who looked at it."

Dan thought he understood, but wanted clarification. "What did you mean when you said it helps you keep the future in mind?"

"It reminds you to think ahead, to train your brain to consider the consequences of your actions. That's not easy, your brain is still learning how to do that. It needs a lot of practice with reasoning, planning, and judgment. After a while, your decisions both on the field and off will become more automatic."

"You mean like a muscle memory?"

"Something like that. With practice, you'll use good judgment and do the right thing without even seeming to think about it. You'll see."

"I hate losing a game because I've done something stupid. It's a real downer."

Mr. Bloomstack nodded. "Just make a mental note about how you'll do things differently next time and then move on. All the moping in the world won't change the past. You need to focus on your next opportunity."

"I'm getting better at that," Dan admitted.

"It's like most things in life; it's amazing what you'll be able to accomplish with a little practice.... You haven't had a chance to explore the wall behind me."

Dan took that as an invitation and walked around Mr. Bloomstack to a wall that looked like a book standing on end with its pages fanned out. He realized they moved, kind of like those racks that hold big rugs in furniture stores. He moved several and saw posters, pictures, medals, buttons, and game uniforms. "Mr. B., what's your favorite thing?"

"That's like asking a parent which is their favorite child. I couldn't possibly choose just one."

"Okay, what are some of your favorites?"

"How about that game jersey you're standing in front of right now?"

Dan looked at the cream-colored jersey with a big blue "A" on it. Inside was the name "Grove" embroidered in red. "Who was Grove? I've never heard of him."

"Never heard of him, never heard of him.... Why Robert Moses Grove, better known as 'Lefty' Grove, was the greatest pitcher who ever lived. That's his 1931 World Series Philadelphia Athletics Jersey. His record was 31-4 that season. He also led in shutouts, strikeouts, ERA, and completed games that year."

"How come I've never heard of him then?"

"I imagine there are hundreds of great players you've never heard of. You need to get back into baseball history. You'll be amazed at what you'll discover." With that, Mr. Bloomstack got up, walked across the room to the wall of drawers. He opened one and took out two pairs of thin, white cotton gloves. He put on one pair and handed the second pair to Dan. "These drawers hold archival documents. When we play with these toys we pretend we're in a museum."

"You call documents 'toys'?" Dan's voice was tinged with condescension. Then he realized he wasn't focused on his next opportunity.

Mr. Bloomstack ignored Dan's tone. "Sure. Toys are all about sparking your imagination. That's what these documents can do. Look at this one." Mr. Bloomstack took a black envelope from a drawer and carried it to the table. He opened it, and ever so gently removed and unfolded an old newspaper.

"This newspaper is one of my most valuable toys. Look at the date on this, 'Saturday April 19, 1947.' I was still wearing diapers back then."

Dan chuckled, "You in diapers? Now that does spark my imagination."

"Now listen up, this newspaper connects some of the most famous names in baseball history: Jackie Robinson, Branch Rickey, Leo Durocher, the Brooklyn Dodgers, Ebbets Field, Wendell Smith, and the Pittsburgh Courier."

"The Dodgers are in Los Angeles."

"They are today, but in 1947 they were in Brooklyn, New York, and they were part of one of the most important events in the history of baseball. Put on your white gloves and take a look at this newspaper. It originally cost 10 cents; you couldn't buy it today for 10,000 times that."

"I'm not sure I want to touch anything that valuable."

Mr. Bloomstack put his finger under Dan's chin and looked him direct in the eye. "I invited you to hold this valuable bit of history in you hands because I know you have both the skill and attitude to treat it as it should be treated. I have no doubts, and neither should you."

Dan gently slipped the newspaper from its acid free folder. It was an edition of the *Washington Afro American.* The big, bold, red headline read, "Brooklyn Signs Jackie Robinson." Dan had never seen a red headline before. It gave him an idea of how important this was to the black community, and how proud they were of Jackie Robinson's accomplishment. He read the article out loud. When he finished he carefully folded the newspaper, placed it back in the folder, and returned the folder to the drawer.

Mr. Bloomstack smiled. "It's impressive, isn't it? Back then, they called that 'The Great Experiment.'"

"How did the experiment work?"

"That's for me to know ..."

"... and for me to find out," Dan completed Mr. Bloomstack's sentence.

"You got it. I think you'll enjoy doing your own research. I know I found it powerfully interesting. You might want to discover what led up to that big day, and what followed it. I tried to imagine what it might have been like for all the members of that team. What it might have felt like to walk in each man's shoes."

"How did it feel?"

"There was a lot of emotion, both good and bad, but the bottom line is we all have a lot to thank that team for."

CHAPTER EIGHTEEN
PAIRED COMPARISONS

"What do you know about baseball cards?" Mr. Bloomstack crossed over to a bookcase and pulled from the shelf a crimson notebook with a large 'R' on the spine. He flipped the pages to a section that displayed a dozen or more Jackie Robinson baseball cards. Pointing to one on a page by itself, he said, "This was my first Robinson card."

Dan studied the baseball card, and then read the yellowing index card next to it. It was printed in a child's hand. The first line read, 'Jackie Robinson Rookie Card.' The second line read, 'Stephen Singer, third grade.' The last line read, 'Traded a Boog Powell card.'

Mr. Bloomstack looked over Dan's shoulder and chuckled. "I'd say old Steve didn't make a very good trade."

"How was Steve to know? He was only in the third grade."

"If you don't know the value of what you have, you're at the mercy of the guy who does." Mr. Bloomstack patted the book. "If old Steve came up those stairs right now and wanted to trade back my original Boog Powell card, I'd be willing to swap him two Jackie Robinson cards for it."

"Jeez, that doesn't sound like you'd be making a good trade to me."

"A Boog Powell card may not be worth much money-wise, but that particular card has a lot of sentimental value for me."

"If you're talking sentimental value, I'd think you'd want to keep your first Jackie Robinson card. Besides, you said it was a rookie card. That should be worth big bucks. I sure wouldn't trade it."

"Hold on there just one little minute. You're jumping to conclusions. If you're going to be a successful trader, you have to be precise in your language and your thinking. I said I'd trade two Jackie Robinson cards for my original Boog Powell card. I never said which Jackie Robinson cards I'd trade."

"Okay, but if this was my collection, I wouldn't know which card to trade. There are pages of them."

"Right. Here is something to remember. You can always make a choice when you can't make a decision."

"That sounds like a bunch of gobbledegook. If you make a choice, you have made a decision."

"Hold on here. You're the one who just said you couldn't make a decision about which Jackie Robinson card to trade. What I'm saying is a lot of small choices can help you make a big decision. It's a technique called paired comparisons."

Dan waited to hear more, but Mr. Bloomstack just flipped the pages of his notebook. Dan tried to wait him out, but finally blurted out, "So what's a paired comparison?"

"That's for me ..."

"Not again!"

"You don't need me. Work on it; you can reason it out."

"Thanks a lot." Dan knew that a pair was two, and that comparison meant looking for similarities and differences. "Will you tell me if I'm right?"

"Absolutely."

"Okay then. I'm guessing that paired comparisons means, you would look at two Jackie Robinson cards at a time and decide which one was the best."

"You got it," Mr. Bloomstack tousled Dan's hair. "See, I told you, you didn't need me. You figured it out on your own. If you repeat that process until you've looked at all of your options, you'll reach a decision."

"With all your Jackie Robinson cards, that could take forever."

"Just for fun, why don't you choose the two Jackie Robinson cards that I should trade if Stephen Singer suddenly appeared on those stairs holding my original Boog Powell card. Start by taking the pages out of the notebook and lining them up on the table."

Dan did just that. Mr. Bloomstack then asked, "Now, if this was your collection, do you see any cards you definitely would not trade?"

"I wouldn't swap any of them unless I had a duplicate."

"That's good reasoning. You just made your first choice using paired comparisons."

"I haven't compared any of the cards yet."

"You just told me you wouldn't swap unless you had a duplicate. So mentally you had *two* sets of cards. One set of cards with duplicates and one set of cards without duplicates. You made a *choice* to trade only cards that had a duplicate. That's a paired comparison in my book. So how many duplicates do you find?"

Dan identified seven different styles of Jackie Robinson cards with multiples.

"How about that." Mr. Bloomstack smiled broadly. "You've narrowed it down to seven sets. How many cards is that altogether?"

"Four sets have two cards, two sets have three, and one set has four cards. That's 18 cards altogether."

"What do you imagine your next task will be?"

"Use paired comparisons to get down to the worst card of each set."

"You got it."

Dan exchanged a knuckle POW with Mr. Bloomstack. He looked at the first set of two cards. "This one is in the worst condition," he announced.

"Good. Now read the index card to see if it has a special provenance."

"A special what?"

"Provenance. That means origin or special history. For example, was the card printed for a special event, or did someone famous once own it, or were only a small number of those cards printed? Things like that. I usually mark the index card with a red asterisk if it has a special provenance. Like I did that index card for my first Jackie Robinson card."

"I get it. There's no red asterisk on either card in this set. So I guess it doesn't have an important providence."

"Prov-e-nance," Mr. Bloomstack corrected.

"Whatever," Dan responded. "So this one is a good trade, right?"

"It is definitely the worst card in that set. So it's in the running. Now use the same criteria to compare the cards from your next set until you're down to the worst card in that set."

"What if a card with a torn corner has a special pro-ve-nance, what then?"

"Provenance almost always outranks condition."

"Then shouldn't I look at provenance first?"

"You just made another paired comparison. Good decision."

Dan was catching on to the idea of paired comparisons. He looked for a red asterisk in the remaining sets. Only one card had a provenance. He made a note not to trade that one. Then he went back to the remaining sets and picked the worst card from each set using paired comparisons. He double-checked his choices for each set. "Now do I make paired comparisons between sets?"

"That you do, but the question is what will you compare on? When you had duplicates, you were comparing apples to apples. You no longer have duplicates, so you'll have to find a measure that will let you compare apples and oranges."

"You mean this is a math problem?"

"Yes and no. You're trying to decide which of two cards has the least value. So what besides condition and provenance might give value to a baseball card?"

"What somebody will pay for it?"

"Excellent! Where do you suggest we look for that information?"

"The Internet?"

"Sounds like a plan. Go for it." Mr. Bloomstack handed Dan his wireless keyboard.

Dan was absolutely at home on the Internet. He clicked with accelerated speed. "Zeeks, Mr. B, look at this. Your Robinson Rookie card is worth a small fortune. This is amazing."

Mr. Bloomstack looked at the screen and whistled. "Wait until Sally hears this. When we're finished, why don't you tell her? If I do, she'll think I'm pulling her leg."

Dan smiled and raised an eyebrow. "You expect me to do all the *leg* work and be your *leg*-man, too?"

Mr. Bloomstack considered how he might formulate a double leg pun, but before he could respond, Dan announced, "Looks like these two would be your best trade, Mr. B."

"I agree. Paired comparisons brought you to a sound decision." With that, Mr. Bloomstack pulled an empty notebook from the shelf. He put on his white gloves for a second time and suggested Dan do the same. "These cards are old and fragile. Even clean hands have body oil, so it's a good idea to use white gloves every time you handle them." He carefully extracted the two cards Dan had identified and their histories from their plastic pockets and handed them to Dan. "Put these in this new notebook."

Dan carefully did as he had been told. When he finished Mr. Bloomstack surprised him. "Those cards are now yours. You can keep them, or you can trade them."

"Mr. B, these may be your worst Jackie Robinson cards, but they still have value. Are you sure you want to give them away?"

"I'm not giving them away. I'm investing them in your education. I'm banking that you will want to know more about The Great Experiment. What difference it made to the world. That you'll want to know more about the history of baseball, and that you'll share what you learn with me. That way we'll both be a little bit smarter as a result of my investment."

"Man, Mr. B, you're the best."

"As long as you pay the proper respect to my toys, you're welcome to come up here and play with them." He paused, "In your free time, that is. Speaking of time, I think we've both lost track of it. Sally's gonna have our hides."

Dan pumped his arms. "Yes!" he yelled at the top of his lungs. "You dropped another 'g' and I win. You load the pop machine for the next week."

Mr. Bloomstack frowned and expressed an exaggerated pout. "Is that any way to treat a guy who just gave you two Jackie Robinson baseball cards?"

"Sorry, Mr. B, but you're the guy who's always telling me 'A deal's a deal.'"

CHAPTER NINETEEN
RIVER BEND

The Roughriders had trained to win, they wanted to win, and most importantly, they expected to win. Dan could feel the energy of excitement among his teammates as the team bus inched its way through the heavy traffic toward the playing field. A gigantic sign announced,

Prairie Conference Championship
River Bend vs. Roosevelt

They were almost there. This was the final game before the state championships. In this exhilarating moment, Dan thought of his dad. For the first time there was no pain in that thought, only an inner comfort that came from knowing his father would have been proud of how hard he had worked and how focused and dedicated he had been to reach this opportunity.

It hadn't been easy, and it almost didn't happen. Not because the Roughriders weren't good enough or hadn't earned it, but because in last week's elimination game, the umpire had clearly favored their rivals from Albright.

Thanks to all his coaches, Dan had been able to control his emotions, keep his focus, and get past the umpire's blatant unfairness. Dan had learned to analyze, correct, and most importantly, move on. He discovered he could leave his mistakes, and team errors, behind and concentrate on the task at hand. A biased umpire was something Dan hadn't considered, and it had taken him a couple of innings to leave his resentment behind and move on, but he had done it. He hadn't permitted himself to get rattled or discouraged. He had taken it one step at a time. He kept focused and pitched just as if it had been Mr. Wall behind the plate, and it paid off. They beat Albright in spite of the umpire.

As the bus pulled to a stop, a large crowd of well-wishers greeted them with cheers, noise-makers, banners, and red and black pom-poms. The team boisterously jostled one another as they prepared to depart the bus. Coach Tisdale's whistle pierced the air. There was immediate silence. "This game is business as usual." To emphasize that, he straightened his cap in his usual way, and began his usual chant.

"Who are you?" Coach barked.

"Roosevelt Roughriders," the team responded.

"What's your vision?"

"To be the best we can be."

"... and your values?"

"Honesty! Integrity! Fair play!"

Coach paused. "After our last game, I heard a couple of you plotting revenge against one of the umpires you felt lacked fairness. Remember this: Regardless of the conduct of the opposing team, regardless of the conduct of the crowd, regardless of the conduct of the umpires, Roosevelt Roughriders always, I repeat always, aim to live by our values. Our goal is to play the game fairly, and with honesty and integrity. When we do that, we are *always* winners regardless of the score. Got that?"

Dan looked at Gabby. He knew in his heart of hearts that they would have let the air out of that umpire's tires if they had known which car was his. Listening to Coach's speech, he realized that if they had succeeded with their revenge, they might both be warming the bench at this game. He swallowed hard.

Coach continued. "I want each of you to know I am very pleased with the growth of this team. At the first of the season, I had told you I expected you to bat, field, and make split-second decisions like champions. You have done that. Each of you has worked to be the best you could be. You are a credit to the history of Roosevelt."

Coach Tisdale walked slowly to the back of the bus, calling each player by name, shaking his hand, and looking directly into his eyes. Then he returned to the front of the bus. "I like the competitive fire I see in your eyes. Keep that fire stoked and the conference title will be yours. Let's bring on the heat!" With that, he pushed open the bus doors.

The team burst onto the field with the force of a flame-thrower. Their crimson uniforms blazed in the Saturday afternoon sun. In his mind, Dan heard his dad's voice: "Attitude is a decision." He felt extra power in his step.

Roosevelt's warm-up was business as usual, just as Coach Tisdale had directed. To keep distractions to a minimum, Mr. Bloomstack and the guys from the Men's League stood at the gates to the field and encouraged reporters and photographers to wait until after the game for interviews. Dan knew the media was watching him, but he resisted the urge to show off. He remembered showing off was what had ended Mr. Bloomstack's pitching career. He took it slow and easy until his muscles were properly conditioned. When a reporter shouted over the fence asking him to demonstrate 'what he had' for the 6 o'clock news, Dan nodded, smiled and hurled the ball to Gabby. He showed good form, but he didn't put his full power behind it. He was saving his strength for when it mattered.

The varsity team took its responsibilities as assistant coaches seriously. They had chartered their own bus to be at this game to help with warm-ups and to cheer on their protégées. Carlsen watched Dan's warm-up approvingly, and held his jacket for him when he finished. The two stood shoulder to shoulder near the dugout, looking at the action on the field and waiting for the game to start. A couple of varsity guys were batting flies and grounders to the outfield. Chandler was looking sharp. His long legs carried him across the field like a gazelle, and when he threw the ball back, his entire body propelled it. Dan watched in admiration. Chandler's throws always had been right on target, but since he joined Dan in taking Madeline Hutchinson's classes, his power and speed had become phenomenal.

On the infield, the players moved with deliberate precision. They snatched line drives and grounders and shot them around the bases with such speed that when the ball connected with a mitt, it sounded like a cherry bomb exploding.

Carlsen nudged Dan, "You have a powerful team behind you, Big D. They're definitely showing a winning attitude."

"Yeah, they're awesome."

The umpire yelled, "Play ball."

The fabulous four hit the bench. Chandler smirked, "Check out that River Bend pitcher's swagger. Man, he's overacting. I think we have him intimidated."

"Or he's just full of himself," Spider said.

"Ya think?" Gabby stepped to the edge of the dugout and began to chatter. "Hey Romano, like the swing of your hips, what color's the bow under your cap." He smiled toward the bench. "That ought to rile him."

Coach Tisdale snapped. "That's enough Sullivan. Take your seat."

Gabby collapsed onto the bench, and put his head in his hands. His voice cracked. "Me and my big mouth. Does that mean I'm benched?" he asked no one in particular.

Spider responded. "You were stupid, but I don't think you broke any of Coach's rules."

Chandler eyeballed Gabby. "Integrity has no need of rules. Remember the poster in the locker room?"

Gabby shook his head, acknowledging his own stupidity. "Yeah, I remember, and the one next to it says, 'Rules cannot take the place of character.'" He paused, then added, "I'm cooked; I just wasn't thinking."

Chandler was back in his face. "Look man, don't give me that. You can control your mouth if you want to. You're a catcher; you make split-second decisions with every play. You can certainly make a split-second decision to be positive or keep your trap shut if you put your mind to it."

Dan put his arm around Gabby's shoulder. "Tell Coach you're sorry right away. Tell him you know what you said wasn't sportsmanlike, and it won't happen again. Tell him you'll keep positive the rest of the game."

Gabby raised his head hopefully. "Ya think?"

Spider pulled him up by the arm. "Ya gotta try, man."

Gabby sidled up next to Coach Tisdale and waited for a change of batters. "Coach, I realize I had a lapse of sportsmanship a minute ago. It won't happen again, I'll keep my chatter positive for the rest of the game. Promise."

Coach Tisdale didn't take his eyes off the field. "See that you do."

Gabby waited to hear more, but no more was said. He walked back to his seat.

"Do you get to play?" Dan wanted to know.

"I'm not sure. He didn't really say."

"Okay, then don't force it, don't ask," Dan advised. "Be presumptive. Take to the field with the rest of us. If he doesn't call you back, you're playing."

At the bottom of the first inning, the Roughriders scrambled from the dugout. Gabby picked up his mask and mitt and headed for home plate. Coach Tisdale didn't call him back. Dan felt his energy surge as Gabby chattered behind home plate. The teams were well matched. The scoreboard continued to rack up '0's for three innings, then at the top of the fourth the River Bend pitcher began to tire. Roosevelt managed a one-run lead.

River Bend tied the game in the bottom of the sixth. Roosevelt came back by two at the top of the seventh. Then at the bottom of the eighth, with two outs, a River Bend batter hit a home run with a runner on first and second.

Their fans went wild. For a moment, Dan felt weak in the knees, then as if on automatic, Carlsen's mantra took over. 'Analyze, correct, move on. Analyze, correct, move on. Analyze …' He was back in his winning mind. When the River Bend batter stepped into the box, it was like a whole new ball game, a clean slate, a new opportunity.

Three beautiful pitches into the strike zone. Dan closed the eighth with a perfect strikeout.

As they came off the field, Coach Tisdale smiled. "I like your body language, men, I can see your resilience in every step. Resilience—that's what makes champions. Champions know how to shed inflated egos when they're ahead, and they know how to bounce back when they're behind. You look like champions to me. You can bounce back. Are you with me?"

"Yes, sir!"

"We need to implement situational hitting. Are each of you prepared to make the sacrifice?"

"Yes, sir!"

"Spider, you're up first. This won't help your home run stats, but we can't risk a fly out. Your job is to get on base. See if you can hit a ground ball near second. They have a weak spot there. Their second baseman is playing wide toward first."

Spider was able to place-hit the third pitch just as Coach had instructed, and with his speed he made first with time to spare. Ethan Feldman was next. Thanks to his sharp eyes, he pulled a walk from a three-two count.

Gabby was up next. Dan had heard Coach Tisdale tell him to sacrifice toward right field, but he wasn't sure Gabby could keep his ego under control. He knew the glory of hitting a home run with two men on base would certainly be more appealing to Gabby's vision of himself than making a sacrifice. Dan thought about the consequences if Gabby did go for the power hit. They would take the lead and most likely win this game, but Coach would most certainly bench Gabby at the State Championship. Dan desperately wanted to advise Gabby, but there was no way of doing that. He could only stand on the side-lines and watch nervously as Gabby came to the plate.

River Bend tightened the infield just a bit preparing for a possible bunt. On the first pitch, Gabby shortened his bat as if he were going to bunt, but let the ball pass. Dan smiled; he should have had more faith in Gabby. He should have known he would put his ego in check when it came to the team. Dan shouted, "Way to go, Gabby. Way to go."

The River Bend players moved two steps closer. The next pitch crossed the outside third of the plate. Gabby calculated, and purposely swung late, hitting the ball to-ward the right side of the field to give Spider time to get to third base. River Bend had been expecting Gabby's sacri-fice, but they had prepared for a bunt, not a short line drive. The ball passed between the first and second base-man. Gabby was safe at first. He couldn't believe his luck. He had expected to be out. He jumped up and down on first base and his chatter went wild. "Yes! Yes! Yes! Yes! Here we go! Here we go! Keep it goin'! Keep it goin'!"

Dan was the next batter. As he approached the plate, Gabby continued his chatter. "You're the man, Big D. You're the man! Bring him home! Bring him home! Take your time, take your time. Choose the one you want! Bring him home! Bring him home!"

Coach had instructed Dan to try to hit over the first baseman's head and short into right field. Dan connected with the second pitch, but not as he had hoped. The ball tipped off the top of his bat for a high popup. It was caught by the first baseman who tagged the base and snapped the ball home. Dan was out, but his sacrifice paid off. Spider had left third the second Dan's bat had connected with the ball; he was home easy. The game was once again tied.

Second baseman Jack Chen entered the batter's box, with Feldman on third and Gabby on second. The River Bend infield was still playing close in. The first pitch came in high in the strike zone. Chen connected for a sacrifice high fly to right field. Gabby advanced to third, and Feldman slid home for a 5-4 one-run lead. The Roosevelt fans roared, and the entire team poured out of the dugout to congratulate Feldman.

The Roughriders had once again demonstrated their resilience. Chandler came to bat with two outs. In response to his reputation for home runs, the River Bend infielders backed up, and the outfielders shifted left and played deep. Chandler, however, wasn't thinking home run. He had his orders. His job was to get Gabby home and get himself to first base without an out.

It became clear that the River Bend pitcher wasn't going to take a chance on a possible home run. It seemed to be his intention to walk Chandler, and take his chances with Stan Sedlacek, who was on deck. Chandler, however, wasn't buying a walk. As the fourth ball came in low outside, Chandler stepped into it and put a low fly over the shortstop's head and into the big hole in the outfield. Gabby scored and Chandler was safe at first. The Roughrider's were now up by two.

From the bench, Dan studied the River Bend pitcher. His shoulders were rounded. He looked tired, yet as Sedlacek entered the box, his bearing changed. He seemed to reach down inside himself and pull things together. He placed his next three pitches in the strike zone, ending the top of the ninth with Chandler stranded on first. Dan secretly admired his adversary's mettle.

As the Roughriders took the field, Dan patted Chandler on the shoulder. "Man, your hours of place-hitting paid off today."

Chandler's smile was huge. "Bottom of the ninth, Big D. Let's bring on the heat!"

The Roughriders were breathing fire. Spider caught an infield fly for the first out. Dan struck out the second batter, and Chandler made a spectacular catch in centerfield for the final out of the game.

The varsity team, fellow students, parents, and fans flooded onto the field. They were jubilant. Dan enjoyed the congratulations and pats on the back. He was surprised to be asked to sign a baseball card with his picture and name on one side, and 'Roosevelt Roughriders Prairie Conference Champions' printed on the other. He asked where it came from, and the kid pointed to the bleachers. He saw Mr. Bloomstack with a crowd of kids around him. Dan knew he was going to have to check that out. He hadn't known a thing about these pictures. Mr. Bloomstack was full of surprises.

The man on the loudspeaker kept asking people to clear the diamond for the awards ceremony. The crowd was not complying. Suddenly, the Star Spangled Banner blared over the loudspeaker. The field quieted for only as long as the song lasted, then the cheers erupted and the celebration continued. After another five minutes of festivity, Coach Tisdale blew his whistle. The Roughriders immediately lined up in front of their dugout, the fans went back to the bleachers, and the awards ceremony took place.

On the bus ride back to Roosevelt, Dan realized the real prize was not the conference championship or the trophy. It was being a member of a team of dedicated and resilient athletes: A true team, where each player was willing to sacrifice his personal glory for the team's success. He could hear Gabby chattering in the seat behind him, "We're Good! Real Good!"

CHAPTER TWENTY
SEASON'S END

Monday morning Dan arrived at the concession stand early. He intended to get in a little practice with Mr. Wall before work. He was surprised to find Mr. Bloomstack already there.

"Morning Mr. B. You're here early."

"Yes, sir-ree-bob, I'm getting a head start on the end-of-the-season inventory."

Dan chuckled. Mr. B really had some strange slang. He was about to ask what it meant, but Mr. Bloomstack continued, "Was that a game Saturday, or was that a game? You boys looked like state champions to me."

Dan stood tall and squared his shoulders. "Hope we prove you right."

"You will, just keep playing like you've been playing. I can imagine your team picture on the front page above the centerfold right now."

"Speaking of pictures, those baseball cards you made were really something."

"I didn't make any baseball cards."

"You can't keep it a secret. One of the kids who asked for my autograph pointed you out when I asked him where he got it."

"That must have been a case of mistaken identity."

"I saw you with a bunch of kids gathered around you."

"That wasn't me they were gathered around. They were gathered around the girl who was selling the cards. I was just a customer."

"The cards weren't yours?"

"Nope. I was just buying a new toy, so to speak." He walked over to a shelf and picked up a protective sleeve into which he had put a set of the Roosevelt player cards. He handed the sleeve to Dan. "I could see you were busy meeting your fans, so I bought an extra set. You can have them for the $5 I paid, plus a quarter for my effort."

Dan laughed. "You're something else, Mr. B."

"Have to set a good example."

"I don't have an extra five with me, but if you'll save them, I'll pay you tomorrow."

"I think I can manage that."

Dan looked at the cards Mr. Bloomstack had handed him. "What if we hadn't won?"

"Then I imagine she would have opened a different box of cards with pictures of the River Bend players."

"Yeah, I suppose. These look really professional. I wonder how she got my picture?"

"Good question. Her business card is there on the table. Why don't you give her a call and find out?"

"That's a good idea. I could buy direct and save a quarter."

"That's how you're going to play the game, is it?"

"No, Mr. B. just teasing, we've made our deal. I'm a man of my word."

"That's reassuring, I enjoyed talking to her, mighty interesting little gal; smart, talented, and a terrific young entrepreneur. I think the two of you might have a lot to talk about."

"You aren't trying to … what is it your generation calls it … match-make are you?"

"No, not me. Never." With that Mr. Bloomstack got out a ladder and set it up. "Glad you got here early, that will give us a head start on our inventory count."

"I came early to practice with Mr. Wall."

"That's my boy. You have your priorities straight. The inventory can wait."

Dan walked over and picked up the business card from the table and keyed the information into his Blackberry. He admired the card. It felt smooth to his fingers, and had a faint smell of perfume. The girl's name was Heather, Heather Sanderson, and her picture was gorgeous. He particularly liked her red hair. He knew he would call her as soon as he got off work. He might even invite her to join the guys Thursday night for the final game of the Men's League. He placed the card on the table, and went out to visit Mr. Wall.

When he finished practice, Dan joined Mr. Bloomstack in the supply room. They worked side-by-side getting a head start on the season-closing inventory. Dan did the counting and Mr. Bloomstack recorded the count on an inventory card, which Dan then attached to each box.

The idea was that if anyone took supplies from the storage room before the concession stand closed, they would change the inventory card to reflect that. Then on Monday, all they would have to do is collect the inventory cards and make the entries in the computer. Mr. Bloomstack's cash register kept a day-to-day running tally of his sales, so he knew what his inventory should be, but as he explained to Dan, he always made an actual hand count on the day of closing to reconcile his figures.

Mr. Bloomstack had been cutting back on reordering supplies for the last couple of weeks, so taking inventory didn't take too long. Dan had decided Mr. Bloomstack wanted his money working for him all winter, not sitting on the shelf tied up in inventory. As Dan stuck the final inventory card to an unopened carton of potato chips, Mr. Bloomstack shouted to his wife. "Sally, we'll just wash up, and then we'll be ready for those chili dogs, baked beans, and potato salad you planned for lunch."

"It will be at the table before you are," she shouted back.

As the three sat at the conference table eating their lunch, Mr. Bloomstack looked at Dan. "Have you decided what you'll be doing when we close shop here?"

"No, not really. I considered yard work and newspaper delivery, the kinds of things Grant did at my age, but none of that really appeals to me."

"What would appeal to you?"

"I thought about starting my own business, but Grant told me that 90 percent of start-ups are out of business in 10 years. Those odds don't appeal to me."

"That's only a half-truth."

"Wikipedia says the vast majority of new businesses fail in the first year."

"That is true. A lot of people are so in love with their idea for a business, they don't do their research and planning before putting their money at risk. Did the Internet also tell you that 90 percent of the entrepreneurs with good business plans and sound operating systems succeed?"

"Those odds sound a whole lot better!"

"Any business will always have risks. However, there's a world of difference between risk and calculated risk. A smart entrepreneur takes calculated risks. You have to balance passion with practicality. It's not enough to start a business that you enjoy, and work hard at it; you have to be selling a product or service people need or want. If there is a market, you're halfway there."

"Only halfway?"

Mr. Bloomstack put his elbows on the table and rolled his right fist around in the palm of his left hand, the way he did when he was getting ready to set you straight. "Well, just because there is a market, doesn't mean the market is there for you. Whatever business you choose, you have to have the basic talent and experience to succeed at it. I remember a guy came to me once wanting me to invest in his restaurant. He was a good amateur cook, but he knew nothing about the restaurant business, never even worked in one. He never had an employee, never managed anything. There was definitely a market for a restaurant and he had cooking talent, but he lacked basic experience."

"So what you're sayin' is that if I have a good business plan, good systems, talent, and experience, I will have a 90 percent chance to succeed?"

"And I'd advise you to have a good brain trust also. That would help you better your odds even more."

"You mean if I'm smart and trust myself?"

"Not exactly, though it does help to be smart and have confidence. But, a brain trust is a group of people who have experience you don't yet have, and they're willing to share that experience with you. They help you to think through your plans and operations. Think of them as a group of business coaches."

"So you're part of my brain trust, right Mr. B.?"

"If you trust my ideas and give them consideration before you act, then I guess I'm part of your brain trust."

"You think I should take what you call a calculated risk and go into some kinda business?"

"It doesn't matter what I think. What do you think?"

"I think I can succeed," Dan said with confidence.

"I'm sure you will. As I said before, you show me a good plan and I'm ready to invest in you. But, I imagine most of your thoughts these days are on the State Tournament. It's only a little more than a week away. Are you getting in enough practice?"

"Yeah, Coach Tisdale says I'm to stick to my regular schedule and keep things as normal as possible."

"Good man, Coach Tisdale."

Sally Bloomstack, who seemed to have her mind elsewhere for most of lunch, pushed her chair back. "Well, this week is not normal for me. I'm over my head with extra things to be done before we start our big road trip Wednesday. Can you two get along without me for the rest of the day?"

"We'll manage," Mr. Bloomstack said. "Dan can work with me in the service area. We'll forget about the outlying diamonds for today."

Dan agreed. "It will be fun to work in the service area, but I could call my old sales team to work the outlying diamonds if you'd like."

Sally kissed Mr. Bloomstack on the top of the head. "That sounds like an A1 plan to me, what do you think Ralph?"

"Be my guest." Mr. Bloomstack flipped Dan his cell phone, then he put his arm around his wife's shoulders and walked her to the car.

When he returned Dan reported, "The guys will be here at 3 o'clock, but what's this road trip thing? I thought you were planning to come watch me at the state tournament."

"I'll be there. Des Moines will be our first stop to check on how our franchisees are doing."

"You have franchisees? Are you sayin' there's more than one Ralph's ?"

"Counting the 3 that we opened this summer, there are now 72 Ralph's in ballparks across the country."

"Whoa! You're full of surprises, Mr. B. I've been working here most of the summer, and I never knew that about you. That's wild. No wonder your clubhouse has so many toys. You must be worth megabucks."

"Well, that depends upon how you define megabucks. My Ralph's bottom line looks good. The concessions make a lot more money than I need for my lifestyle, but that money's not just sitting around. I put it to work, so I'm not very liquid. Most of that money is tied up in venture capital."

"What's adventure capital?"

"Venture, not adventure, but you're right, it sometimes feels like an adventure. A venture capitalist is someone who puts money in a start-up business in exchange for some equity shares in the business. If the business I invest in succeeds, I usually make a pretty good return on investment. As a shareholder, I don't have any liability for debt, but if there is a profit, I will receive my fair share. The return doesn't come right away, mind you. New businesses have start-up costs, and it usually takes a while before they show a profit. However, if they don't show a profit when they should, I shut them down."

"You mean put them out of business."

"Do you stop playing baseball just because you lose a game? Does Coach Tisdale kick you off the team just because you didn't pitch a winning game?"

"No," Dan said, "He has me analyze what went wrong and take steps to correct the problem."

"Well, I do the same. My real investment is in people. Unless they're crooked, I never put *them* out of business. I just put them out of *that* business. There's no shame in closing a business that isn't giving you the return on investment you think it should."

"Have you closed a lotta businesses?"

"Not many. I invest in Main Street, not Wall Street. I know the Main Street marketplace pretty well, and I make sure there is a good business plan and systems in place, and that the person I'm investing in is a good decision maker and has talent and experience."

"Speaking of experience, Mr. B., I don't have any. I've never run a business. Why would you invest in me?"

"You might not be ready to run Ford Motor Co., but you have a great deal of experience to start your first small business. You've created a project plan, and that's pretty similar to a business plan, you've learned about negotiation, advertising, marketing, sales, you even trained a sales team. They may not have been employees in the true sense, but they worked for you. You supervised them."

"Yeah, and I've learned about shipments and stocking, and after this morning, I pretty much understand inventorying. I guess I do have some experience after all."

"You won't succeed at just any business, but you will succeed if you choose a business that is equal to your talent, experience, …"

"… and if customers want what I'm selling and I have a sound business plan and systems."

"You got it. We have an hour before we have to open the concession stand. What do you say we go up to the club house for awhile?"

Dan scrunched his paper napkin and the remains of his hot dog wrapper into a ball and tossed it in the waste can. "I'm for that. My research on Jackie Robinson is goin' gangbusters."

CHAPTER TWENTY-ONE
THE YOUNG ENTREPRENEUR

Dan debated with himself half the day. Should he email Heather Sanderson, call her on the phone, or ring her doorbell? In the end, he decided he needed some big brother advice. He activated his email.

Grant,
There's this girl from Wilson I want to meet. Should I email, phone, or ring her doorbell? What do I say?

Who is she? Why do you want to meet her?

Her name is Heather Sanderson. She was selling baseball cards with pictures of our team at our conference championship. Mr. Bloomstack met her. He says she is smart, talented, and is a terrific entrepreneur. Her picture is on her business card. She's gorgeous.

Phone her. You'll hear the tone and inflections of her voice. It's more personal than email. Forget the doorbell. If she is not expecting company, it could be embarrassing for her, and you. True, you don't know much about her, but I think you can create a pretty good sales pitch from the little you've told me.

Sales pitch? I don't want to sell her anything.

Bull! You're trying to sell her on you. You understand AIDA and negotiation. Just put what you already know to work.

Forget it. You make it sound crass and manipulative.

Manipulation is getting what you want at the expense of the other person. Remember, successful negotiation is about both sides getting what they want. Using your skills is not manipulative. It's common sense. When you're pitching, you know better skills mean better results. It's the same here, better skills mean better results.

Selling "me" still doesn't sound good. I'm not that kind of person.

Come on, you sell yourself everyday. Be honest. Did you think about how you dressed this morning? You were packaging "you." Your clothes and hairstyle advertise who you are. Every conversation you have, either you or the other person is probably trying to sell an idea: To go somewhere, to do something, or just agree with what's being said. I'm trying to sell you an idea right now.

I'm not sure I'm buying.

That's up to you. Gotta go! Have a date myself. Just remember, sales and negotiation techniques are like any other tool. They can be used for good or bad. It's true some people use good techniques for bad purposes, but don't blame the techniques. Keep me posted. ☺

Dan turned away from his computer, picked up his baseball, and flopped across his bed. He tossed the baseball rhythmically back and forth. He thought a mantra might help, but none came to mind. He was uncomfortable with what Grant had said about selling himself, but he couldn't put his finger on why. He realized he shouldn't dismiss Grant's advice without knowing why it was not for him. He decided to think it through. If he used AIDA when he called Heather, how would he do it?

He would have to get her attention. Calling her on the phone would do that. What would arouse her interest? He figured talking about her baseball cards might do it, and that was something he intended to do anyway. What would raise her desire? He thought of two possibilities: first, he did want to buy another set of the Roosevelt cards, and he also wanted to hear all the who, what, where, when, why, how, how much, how many, and how long about her business.

Dan saw that using AIDA to sell himself was essentially a form of planning ahead. The only thing left was what his call to action would be. He could invite her to Jimmy's, but they probably wouldn't have much privacy to talk. He could invite her to a hangout near her school, but that would have the same problem.

He finally settled on two coffee houses downtown. That way, if she decided to meet with him she wouldn't have to make a decision about where. Dan knew from paired comparisons that a choice was always easier than a decision. He went to his desk, pulled up a blank screen on his computer and wrote down his talking points, just to make sure he wouldn't strike out if his mind suddenly went blank. Then he picked up the phone and made the call.

Heather selected the coffee shop that was located in the bookstore. Dan purposely arrived a good 10 minutes early for their meeting. He browsed the business book section, selected one about young entrepreneurs, sat down in one of the wing back chairs, and began to read while he waited. He knew Grant would call this packaging himself, and he knew he was doing it to make an impression, but he told himself he was also really interested in the book.

"Dan?" Her voice was low and rich.

"Heather." Dan stood to shake her hand. She was even more gorgeous than her picture.

"I'm so glad you called. Your pitching last Saturday was amazing."

"Thanks. River Bend was a tough opponent." Dan was eager to get the attention off himself. "I'm eager to hear about your business. Like I said on the phone, I've been thinking of doing something myself, but I'm not sure what, and I am just starting to study up on it."

"You're smart not to jump in before you have planned it all out."

"Let's get a table and you can tell me about your base-ball card business." Dan put the book he had been looking at on the table and together they climbed the three steps that divided the bookstore from the coffee house. There were only two free tables. The place was filled with college kids, graduate students, and older people. For a moment, Dan felt out of place, but then he realized everyone else was into their own thing and they hadn't even noticed them. They ordered their drinks, and sat down at a small round table near the wall.

Dan looked across into Heather's hazel eyes. The specks of brown, green, and amber were highlighted by her chartreuse T-shirt. He had never really paid much attention to eyes before, but he couldn't stop looking into hers. Was he staring? He had lost his concentration. What had he been saying? He stammered, "So, ah, so just how did you decide to sell baseball cards?"

"I knew I wanted to start a business, but I didn't know exactly what. Mom and Dad both have their own businesses. Mom's a horticulturist; she grows herbs, and Dad has a printing company."

"That explains why your cards look so professional."

"Partly. My interests are photography and graphic design. They kinda come together in the baseball cards."

"Does that mean you took all the pictures for your cards?"

"Um humm."

"I never even knew my picture was being taken."

"That's good. You weren't supposed to know. That was part of my agreement with Coach Tisdale."

"Coach knew all about this?"

"Sure. I had to have an agreement that permitted me to take pictures of your team and print them on my cards."

"That makes sense. I should have thought of that."

"We agreed on 15 percent of my net earnings going to your team. I also agreed not to distract his players. Most of the shots I took using a telephoto lens on my digital camera."

"I still don't see how I could have missed you."

"At games I dressed like the media camera guys. I wore men's clothes and kept my hair under a baseball cap."

"Can't imagine you looking like a guy."

"In grade school I wanted to be an actress. I did a lot with the youth and community theatre. So I'm pretty good with disguises."

"Maybe I saw you in something."

"Maybe. I was Annie in Little Orphan Annie. Did you see that?"

"I did. That was you? You were outstanding. My mom raved about your singing."

Heather smiled and blushed. "The picture that I used on your baseball card I shot from a blind I set up in the hedgerow not far from what you call the *Talking Tree*. You were doing warm-ups along the third base line with Bob Carlsen. I got a good shot of him also."

Dan thought about when he had hidden in the bushes to spy on her school's players, but he didn't think he knew her well enough to talk about that. Instead he said, "You could have probably used your interests in photography and graphic arts in dozens of different types of businesses. Why high school baseball cards?"

"It's a long story. My folks kept telling me I have an entrepreneurial spirit. That helped build my confidence. It took me a couple of years to save my start-up costs. Even after I had my resources, I wasn't sure what business I wanted to try."

Dan understood that. "That's where I am now. Mr. Bloomstack says I would be a good businessman. I have been saving my money, but I have no idea what business I want to go into."

Heather nodded. "I've read a little on the subject and they say whatever business opportunity you choose, you have to be passionate about it. It's a lot of hard work, and there can be disappointments."

"You have a passion for baseball?"

"Not just baseball, I love lots of sports. I'm not very good at them myself, but I enjoy watching and taking pictures of our school teams. A lot of my pictures get published in our school paper and I make posters of those when people ask. That's how I made most of my start-up money."

"So you had a poster business first?"

"It was more like a hobby. The hardest part for me was to realize not every good idea translates into a business opportunity. A good business idea has to be anchored in a customer need or want. You have to know if you have a competitive advantage, and a favorable environment, and your timing has to be right, and most important, you have to have adequate capital."

"I've never seen baseball cards for high school teams," Dan said, "so you definitely have a competitive advantage, particularly since your dad has a printing business. But aren't your customer orders rather limited? I would think no one but Roosevelt students and parents would want Roosevelt baseball cards."

"You're right. I have to be able to produce short runs inexpensively. Right now, my business is designed for a niche market, but I've also designed it so I can grow the business when I'm ready."

Dan saw the big picture. "Yeah, there're lots of high schools in our area. You could expand and do cards for all of the sports teams at each school. There are hundreds of athletes in our region."

Heather nodded. "That's the future. Right now I don't need big orders for my business to succeed. My dad's operation is set up for printing on demand, and it can handle my small orders. I can run just a few cards and still make money. My business is what they call mass customization. My cards are essentially all the same; the only things that change with each order are the pictures and the text."

Dan frowned. "But that's the whole card. What else is there?"

"Well, the difficult part was creating the original templates. That was time-consuming. Now it takes me less than five minutes to change the pictures, text, or swap a different template. My card stock, sizes, and ink are standard for every run. That means the equipment doesn't require any time-consuming adjustments for each new order. Plus, on my dad's equipment, I can fit several different cards on one sheet. By the time I finish a press run, I might have four or five orders done."

"I'd like to see your operation sometime."

"I have an order I'll be printing tonight. You can come with me if you like."

"That sounds great. I'd like that. You mentioned timing. This is the end of the season; the state championships are next week. The baseball season will be over before your business really gets off the ground."

Heather agreed. "You're right. Are you familiar with opinion leaders?"

"Not really."

"They're the hot crowd. The crowd everybody wants to be like. If they wear a new style, everyone has to have it. If they buy some new electronic gadget, everyone has to have it."

"Yeah, I've noticed that."

"Have you noticed the reverse is true also?"

Dan guessed, "If they don't like something, no one else does either?"

"You got it!"

"I'm not sure about that. If I like something, I really don't care much what other people think."

"That's because you *are* an opinion leader. You make up your own mind, but a lot of other kids don't. They just follow you."

Dan looked at her smile and thought, 'I'd follow you anywhere.' But he said, "So, you're saying a start-up business should be paying attention to who their first customers are."

"Right. I wanted to start with the best team in my market. I thought Roosevelt had the best chance to win the conference championship. If I began with the champions, every other school in the conference will want to be just like the champions. Other coaches likely will follow Coach Tisdale's lead, and by the opening games of next season my business should be positioned to score big."

"What if we lose at state, what does that do to your business plan?"

"You won't; you're going to win the state championship. But if you don't, you're still the best in our conference and that is where my business is right now."

It made Dan feel great to know Heather thought Roosevelt would win the state championship.

He knew he was blushing. He could feel his ears heat up. He lost his concentration again. What was it they had been talking about? He moved in a slightly different direction. "My boss Ralph Bloomstack is a big collector of baseball stuff; he bought a couple of your Roosevelt sets Saturday. Maybe he can help you connect with the collector market."

"Ralph Bloomstack ordered an entire case of Roosevelt cards on speculation. That's my print job for tonight."

"Somehow that doesn't surprise me."

Heather gushed, "He's my biggest customer so far. He even bought all the River Bend cards I thought I'd have to shred when they lost. I didn't think they had any value, but Mr. Bloomstack told me that if my cards became collectable, the River Bend cards might have some historical significance. Because they were never sold on the open market, they could become the most valuable of all. That doesn't make sense to me."

"It's a collector thing. It has to do with provenance and rarity. High school baseball cards are a new thing for collectors. Since our conference championship was your company's first event, that's a very special provenance. Then, since you will never print more cards declaring River Bend as conference champions, those cards are a limited edition. That will make them rare."

"My dad collects baseball cards, but I didn't know all that."

"I've just started to collect. Mr. B. is a good teacher."

"Mr. B.?" Heather questioned.

"That's what I call Mr. Bloomstack. It's a long story." Dan noticed Heather had finished her drink. "Would you like a refill?"

"Another time maybe. Say, since you're going to come see my press tonight, why don't you come home to dinner with me? Then Dad can drive us both over to the press."

"That sounds like fun. I'll give Mom a call." Dan could hardly believe his luck. The afternoon had been fantastic, and now he was invited to dinner. Heather Sanderson was everything Mr. Bloomstack had said she was, and much more.

CHAPTER TWENTY-TWO
STEEE...RIKE TWO

"Steee...rike two." Still on his haunches, Gabby snapped the ball to third base. The Madison Creek runner quickly retreated to second. The din of the crowd was energizing the stadium. Dan's emotions were close to the surface, and he struggled to keep them under control. He had never felt so much stress. This was it, the big one—the state championship they had trained and played so hard to reach. The Roughriders had a one run lead in the bottom of the ninth, two outs, a runner on second, and the batter with a three-two count. "Way to go, Big D. You're the man. Way ahead of him. Way ahead of him. One more, we only need one more. The next one's ours." Gabby's chatter was continuous.

Dan stepped off the mound and pawed at the dirt with his cleat. A bead of sweat sent a cool trickle down his back, and he felt his body shiver in response. His right arm ached, but he controlled the impulse to massage it. Carlsen had taught him that body language counted. He had to appear cool and in control.

Dan thought he had learned to ignored hecklers, but right now the high-pitched harangue from the Madison Creek runner on second base was getting to him. He knew it was because he was feeling guilty. He should have never walked the twerp, and there was simply no excuse for letting him steal second. Dan knew he had to focus, yet in his peripheral vision he could see the kid bouncing off and on second base like an Internet pop-up ad.

Gabby sensed there was a problem and jogged out to the mound. "We've got Davidson where we want him. What'cha want to do? A fast ball, low inside?"

"Davidson's swing has the force of a straight-line wind. If he connects with a fast ball, it'll be out of the park."

"Man, he's not going to connect. He's only been batting 120," Gabby countered.

Almost as if he could hear their conversation, Dick Davidson stepped back into the batter's box, swung his bat a couple of times, and smiled directly at them before stepping out and casually tapping his bat against his cleats.

Dan studied him, trying to decide if Davidson was confident or just cocky. "It only takes one. He's lookin' pretty relaxed."

Gabby was incredulous. "Man, what'cha thinkin'? Ya know Davidson can't take the pressure. You can out-psych him, like easy."

Dan felt goose bumps on the back of his neck and momentarily considered walking Davidson. Then he looked over to see Rob Reilly selecting his bat. Reilly had the highest batting average in the state. It was no contest. Dan knew he had to stand up to Davidson. He had to deliver a pitch to the strike zone knowing it will be a do or die ... for him, or for Davidson. One of them will walk away a hero. The other will ... Dan didn't finish the thought.

There was still uneasiness in the pit of his stomach. He let go a little belch to try and avoid the upchuck he felt was threatening. Mr. Bloomstack, who was sitting just behind the Roosevelt dugout, stood up and yelled, "Mind your business." Dan heard the familiar voice above the roar. He looked toward his personal cheering section. Mr. Bloomstack, Grant, his mom, Carlsen, and Heather were all cheering him on. He felt immediately centered. He fully understood what it meant to mind his business. He needed to focus on the goal, check the systems, mind the details, and execute his plan with disciplined precision. Dan looked around the field at his teammates. It was clear their adrenaline was high and they were focused. This *was* business as usual. Dan did some quick paired comparisons.

Realizing Gabby was waiting for a response, Dan replied, "Yeah, yeah, okay, you're right. Be sure and brace yourself, 'cause it's comin' supersonic."

"Way to go, Big D." Gabby high-fived Dan and jogged confidently back to home plate.

Dan scooped up his rosin bag and rubbed it between his palms as he returned to the mound. As he tossed it to the ground, it seemed to carry with it any residue of tension that had been building within him. He knew this would be his final pitch of the season. He nodded to his cheering section. It wasn't a delay tactic exactly; he just wanted to savor the moment and acknowledge their support.

Fans on both sides were on their feet. The crowd was wild with enthusiasm. Dick Davidson entered the batter's box for his final call. He crouched, swung his bat a couple of times, and positioned it above his shoulder. He may have smiled. Dan didn't notice. He was totally focused. It was as if he had muted the entire ballpark with the click of a remote. His concentration was on the baseball in his hand and on Gabby's glove. He felt in complete control. It was exhilarating to be at the top of his game.

With a studied grip, he balanced, pumped twice to confuse Davidson, shifted his weight, kicked high, stretched long, delayed, rotated, and launched the ball. It was perfect. Just where he intended it to be, in the strike zone, low inside. Davidson's powerful body rotated toward the ball. A thunderous metallic crack silenced the crowd. Dan watched in disbelief as the ball passed in a low arc over his head, destined for a big gap in the outfield.

Chandler in center and Spider at shortstop responded. They were each about equal distance from where the ball was headed. The base runner rounded third and headed for home plate. It appeared the ball would evade both Chandler and Spider. Then Chandler's stride miraculously lengthened; he was inches closer than Spider.

Dan could see it was close, but not impossible. Chandler's arm was extended to the maximum. The ball hit the tip of his glove, deflected up, and then began its descent toward the ground. That slight deflection bought the time that Spider needed. He responded more like a gymnast than a baseball player. His body spun horizontally, his right arm extending toward the ball, now only inches from the ground. He landed hard, skidded, and did a somersault that ended with him holding both hands above his head in the typical gymnast climax. The baseball was clearly visible in the web of his glove. The Roughriders had won a spectacular victory!

Dan was ecstatic. He rushed with the rest of the team to put Spider on their shoulders. As he helped lift Spider aloft he felt a spurt of jealousy. Dan had expected to be the hero, the one lofted into the air for everyone, especially Heather, to see. He had minded his business well for the entire season, yet Spider was the hero on a single play. Then the crystal ball flashed across his mind. Its image cleared the jealously from his heart.

The excitement of the moment elated him. He realized that the championship was not about his pitching, or Spider's save. The championship was about the decisions each player had made all season. He felt good about that. Then unexpectedly, Dan felt himself swept off his feet, as Chandler lifted him to his shoulder. He and Spider were both aloft. Gabby was yelling "We're the best, we're the best." Soon the Roosevelt fans joined in unison, "We're the best, we're the best," repeated again and again like a mantra. Heather was running alongside the team taking pictures. Roosevelt had batted like champions, fielded like champions, made decisions like champions, and now they *were* champions. Life was good in the "Strike Zone."

Knowledge is something you can gift, and at the same time keep. Isn't that remarkable?

CLASSIC BOOKS FOR PARENTS

These classic books are powerful. They provide a reservoir of wisdom to sharpen your competitive edge, and assist you to coach your teens effectively in their journey toward maturity and financial security.

Getting to Yes
Roger Fisher and William Ury

How to Win Friends and Influence People
Dale Carnegie

Paradigm Pioneers
Joel Barker

Positioning: The Battle for the Mind
Al Ries and Jack Trout

Rich Dad, Poor Dad
Robert T. Kiyosaki

See You at the Top
Zig Ziglar

Suzi Orman's 2009 Action Plan
Suzi Orman

The Millionaire Next Door
Thomas J. Stanley and William D. Danko

Think and Grow Rich
Napoleon Hill

Note: Although Ralph Bloomstack is a figment of my imagination, the baseball memorabilia in his collection actually exist. See photographs in *Smithsonian Baseball: Inside the World's Finest Private Collections*, complied by Stephen Wong.

ACKNOWLEDGEMENTS

This book is essentially a re-gifting of other people's ideas. Over my lifetime, my parents, family, friends, teachers, coaches, mentors, strangers, books, seminars, movies, and television have all made contributions to the viewpoints I share in this book. I should like to credit each person for their contributions; unfortunately the exact origin of most of the ideas have receded into the mist of time.

The storyline, characters, and dialog are figments of my imagination. As an observer of business, finance, and baseball, I believe the advice I share is sound. If experts find I have misunderstood, or been a bit too creative in adapting ideas to this book, I invite them to set the record straight at S.L.Hudson@StrikeZone-TheBook.com.

Several people have made time in their busy lives to preview this book, in whole or in part. Their feedback has been constructive, and highly valued. My thanks to Lisa Angelella, Ellen Buchanan, Sarah Chicchelly, Dorothy Crum, Tricia DeWall, Magdalena Diamond, Roger Fisher, Deirdre Giesler, Bob Goodfellow, Deb Green, Bradford Hudson, Helen Mapp, Dottie Ray, Sarah Seidl, Mark Trimble, Ocie Trimble, Rich Trolliet, and Robert Wachal. I appreciate their coaching.

As a member of three writers groups, I have had the opportunity to practice, practice, practice. My fellow writers have been "ruthlessly kind" in encouraging me to be the best I can be. My thanks to the Gray Hawk Writers Group, The University Club Writers Group, and the Iowa City Branch of The National League of American Pen Women.

Acknowledgements

Graphic designer Robyn Hepker collaborated to create the cover for this book. She has translated my concept beautifully. Robyn has both skill and finesse. It has been fun and educational working with her.

A gigantic "THANK YOU" is due to John Boswell Hudson. His encouragement and active interest in my writing kept me motivated. He has been a tireless editor. As each chapter was written, John read it orally. He laughed in all the right places, praised my ability to simplify complex concepts, and demonstrated a genuine enjoyment for my storyline. John researched the publishing process, and took the related steps that put this book into your hands. His attention to detail has been major.

My publisher, CreateSpace, has earned kudos for their innovations in publishing.

Life is good in the strike zone,
Iowa City, Iowa
October 2009

S. L. Hudson
EdM, Harvard University

S.L.Hudson@StrikeZone-TheBook.com
www.StrikeZone-TheBook.com

Made in the USA